SERIOUSLY SEXY 1

SERIOUSLY SEXY 1

A collection of twenty erotic stories

Edited by Miranda Forbes

Published by Accent Press Ltd – 2008
ISBN 9781906125820

Printed and bound in the UK

Cover Design by
Red Dot Design

Contents

Seducing Claire
by Penelope Friday

From the first moment I saw Claire, I wanted to seduce her.

Am I too blunt? Let me go further.

I wanted her naked underneath me on a bed, her blonde hair trailing across the pillow, writhing and crying out under my touch. I wanted to see her high, tight breasts exposed, the nipples sharp peaks of wantonness. I wanted to discover whether the thatch of curls protecting her sex were the exact same shade as her hair; and I wanted to bury my mouth beneath them and pleasure her until she could think of nothing but me.

But you can't say that when you're standing on a stranger's doorstep, greeted by a long, querying look; a raised eyebrow. Instead I said,

"Hi, I'm Madeline. I'm the new lodger."

Why, you look surprised. Did it not occur to you that I was female? Have you never looked and lusted over someone of the same sex as you – someone who is the same, yet intriguingly different? If not, I pity you. Claire was – she was not breathtakingly attractive in the usual fashion, but she had a charisma and sensuality that oozed out of every pore. Sharing a house with her, I saw her dressed up to the nines in a knock-out black dress; slumming in front of the television in a pair of old PJs; bleary-eyed as she stumbled out of the door on the morning after a late night. But I never saw her without wanting her.

That first morning she gave a small smile and a nod of comprehension.

"Of course. Come in."

I had not previously seen the room I would be renting. My move down South had been sudden, and the arrangements all made by telephone from Liverpool. If it didn't work out, I had thought, I could always move on. Claire herself had just been a soft pleasant voice on the other end of a phone: I hadn't thought then that I would fall for her in that first moment. Unless the room was impossible, I vowed privately, I would be staying.

It dawned on her only slowly how I felt. For too long, too many aching months, she saw me just as Madeline, her lodger and, later, her friend. And I was patient because – oh, because she was Claire and as I stayed there I found the first desire changing, deepening. I still wanted her (so much) but now I realised I wanted more than simple seduction. I wanted to love and be loved by her; to make her heart sing and her body long for me. But she – she was serenely unaware: unaware of what it did to me when I came down the stairs in the morning to find her ironing a work shirt, dressed only in the skimpiest, sexiest underwear; flicking her hair back over one bare shoulder to keep it out of her way. Claire could never intentionally have been provocative – the very concept would have made her giggle – but in her unconscious sensuality she was almost irresistible.

And she felt comfortable with me: a friend, not a lover – perhaps an advantage when Claire's address-book was filled with men who had let her down. As we sat one evening, a few months into our stay, with the television more background noise than anything else, I saw her eyes fill with tears at her latest disaster, and my heart raged at those who had broken hers.

2

"Claire; Claire, dearest…"

I had not meant to say so much, but as she leaned into my hug, I was unable to stop myself from kissing her, my lips soft on hers. She froze, her eyes checking mine as if in disbelief before she edged away. It had been too soon, too much. I was a fool.

"I'm sorry," I said humbly.

"Madeline…"

She didn't know which question to ask first. Had I meant it? Had I meant it in *that* way? The answers were yes and yes again, but as I nodded I saw her face fill with doubts.

She liked me, yes – but she was only just out of her last (painful) relationship. Worse, I was female. I was an end to her straight female dreams of husband, children, meat and two veg in the evenings. I was complication, confusion, difficulty.

I could have told her that anything was possible, but in the end it all came down to Claire. Whether she wanted me in the same way I wanted her. I could fantasise all I liked, but without Claire's love my dreams would just be a pale shadow of what I really desired.

"It's too…" She wavered for words.

"Yes."

I put my hand on her arm for a brief second, needing that connection; needing my own reassurance as much as she needed hers. Our eyes met again, and I saw the fear in her look and smiled reassuringly at her.

"I know," I whispered. "I'm sorry."

She hesitated a second.

"Maybe…" she said, but then she looked away and hurriedly got to her feet, stumbling to the door and up to her room.

I let her go.

Maybe, she had said. It was better than "no".

*   *   *

3

In the weeks that followed, though, "maybe" was too close to being "no". Her eyes would catch mine and she would look away, hastily. Our intimate discussions were drawn to a close as Claire was "too tired," "going out," "not in the mood". I nodded, and accepted the excuses with every sign of believing them and gradually Claire began to relax around me once more. She smiled when we passed each other on the landing. She bounced in from work to tell me about her promotion. But she made no mention, no sign, of what had been between us. I began to think that she'd forgotten – or worse, that she wanted to forget – that moment. That softly spoken *maybe*.

I sat in my bedroom one early summer evening, watching the birds gather together to roost in the trees, and wanting – just wanting the love, the companionship of one other person. Why not admit it? Of Claire. Suddenly, I heard her voice.

"Madeline?" Claire was calling me from her bedroom. There was something strange about her tone but I couldn't quite think what it was.

"Yes?"

There was a little pause, and then...

"Will you come in?"

I held my breath. It was the first time I'd received such an invitation since – well, since Then. Life with Claire, however much she'd relaxed recently, still felt divided into two: before The Kiss and after. But this invitation held hope; a promise that even if I might not get everything I desired, Claire would at least accept me as a close friend once more. I pushed her door open, and then stood, stunned, in the doorway.

Claire was naked.

She was lying stretched out on her bed, on top of a plain white cotton sheet, and her eyes met mine anxiously.

"Are you sure you meant...?" she asked hesitantly.

"Are *you* sure?"

I could hardly breathe, looking at Claire's beautiful body spread before me. I did not think that I *could* walk away now. She gave me a smile.

"Never surer."

Her hair looked primrose yellow against the white sheet – warm and inviting. I tiptoed across to her side, and ran my fingers through the fine, smooth strands and smelt the familiar scent of Claire's apple conditioner. It reminded me of that first month in the house, hearing the hiss of the shower and being overwhelmed by the temptation of the idea that I might slip through the bathroom door and look – just look – at Claire naked, her breasts and hips dripping with hot water, smoothing shampoo from the roots to the tips of her hair. She would come out, moments later, wrapped in a fluffy towel and smelling of apples. I smiled at the memory.

"What?" Claire murmured, grey eyes on my face.

"You. You're beautiful."

She laughed in happy disbelief. I could have told her a million times how gorgeous she was and she still would not have believed me.

"Then kiss me," she demanded.

It was a request I was delighted to fulfil. Her lips had been cool and uncertain that first time I'd pressed mine to them; now, she gave herself up to me, her mouth teasing, licking, nibbling at my own.

"Maddy... Maddy, darling..."

And oh, my name on her lips. It felt like magic, like the whispered words of a spell. My Claire, keening out my name. I bent my head to nuzzle at her neck, used my tongue to trace her collar bone. She squirmed and giggled, reaching up to pull me on top of her. I was worried about squashing her delicate body, but she told me teasingly that a lightweight like myself could do her no harm, and that she

5

loved the feeling of my skin pressed up against hers. And how could I refuse her anything?

Her legs tangled around mine, taking them prisoner. I looked into her face, watching her happy enjoyment of her own sexuality. She could give me no greater gift. Every trace of doubt had gone from her eyes. She saw what I was thinking and ran possessive fingers up my spine, pushing my shirt over my head with one swift movement.

"Stop psycho-analysing me and get down to business."

"Yes, boss."

I undulated my body against her, enjoying the points of contact, the cool air where we were apart. Hands either side of her face, I kissed and kissed her again, savouring the warmth of her mouth; the sweet-tang taste of her; the essential Claire-ness.

She was a joyful lover, receiving gladly and giving with as much pleasure. Her hands wandered over me as I pressed my lips to her ears, her neck, her breasts. I could feel her heartbeat against mine; and the throbbing in my chest set up a deeper throbbing below, warm and wet.

"Claire – Claire…" I sighed.

Her hands were pushing my trousers from me, gently peeling my underwear off. I wriggled to allow her access, and she made a soft appreciative noise as I touched a sensitive spot.

"You like *that*?" I asked, moving over and again until she squirmed in turn, half-laughing, half-moaning her pleasure. "What about this?"

And fantasy became reality as I knelt between her legs, mouth gentle on her thighs, tongue less gentle on that precious nub beneath the blonde curls. She squealed and wriggled; and I put my hands on her hips to hold her still, so that I could please her the more. She gasped, then put her hands over mine.

"Maddy…"

6

"Mmm?" I lifted my head a little way to look at her.

"Turn round. Let me do the same to you."

The very thought was a turn on. I rolled over so that we were side by side, and we nuzzled at each other until we were both almost too breathless to continue. I had to move away to continue, but I wanted to see Claire come, to see her find the ultimate satisfaction in what I was sharing with her. I flicked my tongue inside her, once, twice and she was gasping and murmuring her satisfaction. I could see her toes scrunched up tightly against the soles of her feet as she orgasmed, every muscle sharing the feeling. I watched as a tear trickled down her face, but when I went to brush it away, her hand caught at mine, and she opened her eyes and smiled.

"You're wonderful," she said softly, pulling me up against her so that we were cuddled together, her warm breath tickling my neck.

Later, she touched and tasted me in turn, her attitude of fascinated new exploration more erotic than any seasoned lover. Her fingers were warm as they delved inside me, her tongue burning as it traced a pattern across my navel until I came, her name on my lips, herself in my heart.

Afterwards, as we lay there in post-coital doziness, I felt her glance across at me, the tiniest smile on her face.

"No regrets?" I asked quietly, my heart aching for the right response.

She shook her head, scrunching up her nose so that the freckles joined to make a pattern, the small smile growing and blooming.

"No regrets."

8

Impressionism
by Jeremy Edwards

Art of the Flash

It had to be deliberate. She couldn't be sitting behind her little art-gallery desk, thighs apart, flashing her neat black panties at me ... by accident.

The shape of the Manhattan art gallery was so long and narrow that from my position in the doorway, the lovely woman at the desk was practically at the vanishing point of my field of vision. Nonetheless, her loveliness, even viewed impressionistically from that distance, was enough to make me stop in my tracks.

I'm quite the art lover – not to mention a mediocre amateur painter – and a woman, no matter how beautiful, is going to have tough competition for my attention if she's surrounded by breathtaking paintings. But this woman had already won that contest, even though her gallery had some of the most engaging pieces I'd seen in many a lunch hour. I was fascinated by her rich black hair, creamy complexion, and sensitive lips. From where I stood, I could not see the personality of her eyes; but I imagined pools of sharp, shimmering intelligence, infused with kindness and garnished with laughing eyelashes.

Her face was sensuous, but her outfit was crisp. An elegant black skirt suit; stockings; and ... oh my ... Nice black panties. Under the desk.

She had to know. She could not work at this desk all day, in the middle of a busy city, and not be aware of when her panties were or were not visible to the casual observer. This really mattered to me. Because, if it were an accident, it would not be polite to let my gaze linger there, or return there between paintings. If, however, it was intentional – as I supposed – then I owed it to both of us to make the most of it.

And then came the question of whether she sat this way all the time, exposing her pantied crotch to the world … or whether she had seen me come in the door, liked the look of me, and given me a special, personal treat. Naturally, I would like to believe that I have such an effect on stunning women. But, in all honesty, I couldn't remember the last time an art-gallery manager had flashed me. Was she an all-purpose exhibitionist, or was she *my* exhibitionist?

I suddenly had the exciting thought that this exquisite woman had been masturbating, alone in the gallery, prior to my arrival. I had interrupted, leaving her horny … and receptive. How I wanted to stroke those receptive panties.

I walked noncommittally toward her end of the shop, and she said, "Good afternoon." And she looked at me with a mischievous expression that told me that, yes, it was deliberate, and, yes, it was just for me.

At this angle, I could no longer see under the desk. But the trade-off was well worth it, because her face was even more beautiful than I had inferred. With such a rare mixture of proportion and personality in her features, she looked like someone who should be immortalized in priceless paintings, not immersed in price-tagged canvases. Perhaps, I reflected, she moonlighted as a model. Had I possessed more talent in that direction, I would have loved to spend countless hours studying her transcendently-serene face and attempting to render it on a canvas. Even with great ability, I conjectured that I would fail to capture her … but what a

10

pleasant way to spend hour after hour failing! I could, I told myself, spend days failing to paint the eyes alone – such deep, sympathetic, clever eyes, imbued with an arresting sexuality. Yes, I had the impression that this was the sort of woman who could discuss the fine points of art history and lewdly flash her underwear, or even her bare cunt, at the same time ... and be passionate about all of it.

I walked even closer to the desk, wordlessly conveying the notion – a not-entirely-false one – that I wanted to get a closer look at a painting in its vicinity. When I stepped within six feet of the lady – my back toward her, as I made a point of facing the art – I detected a subtle, feminine aroma that encouraged me in my hopes that she was aroused by my presence, and had maybe even primed herself with her fingers before I had walked in.

After I'd had my fill of the still life that I had chosen as a diversion, I spun around and grinned at her.

"Nice," I said, in a tone of voice that hovered between public space and bedroom.

She blushed slightly. "Thank you. And I mean it," she explained with warmth. "The gallery works very closely with its artists, and so the compliments their paintings receive are personally meaningful to the woman behind the desk."

The woman behind the desk. The woman with sometimes-visible, perhaps daintily-moistened lingerie.

"Does the woman behind the desk always speak about herself in the third person?" I was taking a chance that she had a sense of humour. Except I wasn't really taking a chance, because I knew instinctively that those eyes held humour.

She smiled agreeably. "It depends what mood she's in." Excellent. Of course a woman like this could keep up with my banter.

"And what mood is she in today?"

11

She shifted in her chair – it was a discreet motion, but its power went straight to my crotch. "Hmm … a good mood, I'm deciding." Her gaze held mine in a gentle but determined grip. "Maybe a restless mood. A glad-to-have-some-company-after-a-boring-morning mood."

I glanced at my watch. "I wish I could stay longer, to enjoy the paintings … and the mood." I again found myself staring directly into those magnetic eyes. "I'll have to pay you another visit when I have more time." I hesitated. "Are you always the one minding the store?"

"Yes, I'll be here for you when you come back." She made another subtle movement in her seat, and I was certain now that she couldn't wait to plunge her hand into her black panties as soon as I was out of the door. "In fact, perhaps you're free tomorrow evening." She picked up a cardstock handbill from a stack on the desk. She scribbled something on it, and offered it to me. I stepped forward to claim it.

"I thought you might like to join us," she said, with an emphasis on the word *join*. "After the close of business tomorrow."

I looked at the card, which advertised the kick-off to a special show featuring some of the contemporary Impressionist painters whose work was displayed here. In a joyful, artistic hand, she had written her name – Valerie – and circled the time, 7:00p.m.

"I think I can make it," I said.

Valerie touched my sleeve. It was a gesture of girlish enthusiasm that was incredibly sexy in the context of her black suit and bustling desk. "I hope you will."

I had to get myself out of there before I impulsively sacrificed a full schedule of meetings to an attempt to get under that desk with those panties. So I took a perfunctory turn around the room, making note of the paintings I'd like to reacquaint myself with later, and then I drifted toward the door. I turned to look at Valerie, who was busy with some paperwork. Her knees were together now. But when my "See you tomorrow" drew her attention my way, I saw them open for me, as if involuntarily.

Walking back toward my office, I imagined Valerie's fingers within her lingerie, her hips rocking in her chair, her eyes closing in ecstasy as she visualized … me? My ordinary-looking face surprised me in a shop window reflection as the fantasy played out in my mind.

By the time I was ascending the elevator, it was obvious that I would need to get inside my own underwear for a minute or two before settling down to the afternoon's work.

As I danced in place in the bathroom, my trousers down to my knees, I could still smell her and see her panties clinging, so very invitingly.

At Her Opening

The gallery door was locked. This was obviously a private affair. I shielded my face from the glare of the streetlights and looked through the window. Right away, Valerie noticed me. She beamed endearingly and let me in.

"I'm so glad you're here …"

"Max," I supplied.

"Welcome to my opening, Max."

I swallowed, because I had already concluded that Valerie was the sort of person whose choice of words was always intentional.

"Let me introduce you to my artists."

I teased her. "'*My* artists', eh? I notice that the woman behind the desk is not in the third person tonight."

Valerie laughed. "Well, for that matter she – *I* – am not actually behind the desk, either."

The next hour was pleasant for all. I had the privilege of admiring the paintings I'd had to rush away from last time, and before long I found myself the proud owner of two of them. The artists bubbled over with enthusiasm in the face of my ready expertise and open wallet. For my part, I welcomed the opportunity to support their genius with my praise and my purchases. As for Valerie, her personal delight at my presence seemed to begin where her professional delight left off.

Nor was I remiss in admiring her. Dressed becomingly in a long peasant skirt and a bohemian blouse, she exuded charm and culture. A hint of lipstick and eye makeup emphasised the radiance of her face, and a drop of Chardonnay brought a pretty touch of colour to her cheeks. (Or was it my company?)

Though she successfully promoted the pleasant illusion that I had her full attention, it was clear that Valerie was no slouch as far as circulating, making introductions, and logging sales where concerned. As the event wound down and I watched her tally up the various artists' lists, I was pleased to note that my two acquisitions represented only a fraction of the evening's transactions.

Soon, even the artists had wished us goodnight, and I was alone with her. I didn't want to risk a faux pas by trying to segue her professional invitation into an intimate situation too abruptly ... but then I remembered that this was a woman who had unceremoniously opened her legs at me.

"Congratulations," I began.

"Thank you," she said. She had been poised all evening. But now that we were by ourselves, she seemed a little shy.

"You've been so busy. You hardly had any wine." I touched her hand for an instant. Her glass, which had never been more than half full, was still a quarter full. "But we can rectify this. Would you help me assess a Bordeaux I've been looking forward to sampling? I live just two blocks from here."

"I'll bring what's left of the cheese," she said smoothly.

The Lady Takes a Seat

Although I have a very comfortable living room, Valerie and I lingered on the chrome barstools in my kitchen, discussing art and travel and wine as we explored the bottle of Bordeaux.

After finishing her second glass, my guest cocked her head in the direction of the powder room. "I'll be right back. I need to go in there and ... sit down for ten seconds." She smiled with a delicate flirtatiousness as she stood up and smoothed her skirt.

"Ten seconds?" I queried amiably, as I escorted her past the stove and refrigerator and opened the door for her. "You're quick!"

"That's what they say," she answered with a wink, and she pulled the door closed.

An instant later, the door re-opened. She couldn't possibly have been *that* quick.

"Umm," she said. "I don't suppose you'd like to accompany me?"

My throat went dry. I could quickly get used to Valerie's brand of private exhibitionism. "You're inviting me to watch?"

"Well, you won't really be able to see anything. I am wearing a long skirt, after all."

But I saw plenty. I saw a beautiful woman gather up enough skirt to expose some fresh thigh flesh above her stockings. I saw her produce black panties – a twin pair to the lingerie I'd met yesterday – from beneath the skirt. I saw her sit with elegance, looking as radiant and dignified as if she were posing for a portrait.

Ten seconds later, we were back at the kitchen counter, polishing off the wine and acting as if nothing had happened, though the air was electric with the fact that it had.

15

Impressions

"Well, Max," she said with husky familiarity. "We've finished all the wine. I've been to the powder room. Now what?" Without waiting for an answer, she leaned in, closed her eyes, and gave my lips a succulent kiss. She tasted as vivid as the fruits in a masterly still life, and she smelled as inviting as a summer seascape. The wine on her breath was like the texture of a ripe peach, beckoning one's tongue. Without even thinking, my hands sought – and found – her chest, and she kissed me more hungrily as I fondled her through her blouse.

Now the kitchen had ceased to be the ideal venue, and we guided ourselves to the living room. There we stood like performers, interlocked before the inanimate audience of two loveseats and a floor lamp.

I didn't even realise how much of her clothing she was shedding while our tongues danced together. When she stepped back, her black panties were all that remained of her outfit. The blouse and long skirt were already at her feet, and, as she peeled the panties, her bra-less breasts swayed for me.

I scurried forward, cradled these breasts anew, and began to kiss their soft flesh, kiss after methodical kiss. "Valerie." *Kiss*. "You have flashed your black panties at me." *Kiss*. "You have said delicious, suggestive things to me and invited me to your party." *Kiss*. "You have encouraged me to join you when you bared your bottom in my powder room." *Kiss*. "And now you stand, naked as a painting and twice as beautiful, in my living room." *Kiss*. "I'm getting the distinct impression ..." *kiss* "... that you're trying to seduce me."

"In the art world, we learn to trust our impressions," she answered.

As she spoke, she pushed my head down gently and began to paint my face, very slowly, with her juicy snatch.

16

Victoria Learns The Arts Of Pleasure
by Angela Meadows

I sat on the bed unfastening my silk stockings and thinking about the evening's events. I wondered what was in store for me at the Venus School for Young Ladies. It looked unlikely to be the demure training for married life that my father had imagined when he sent me away from my beloved Bill.

The door opened and my room-mate Beatrice swept in. Her lace gown was undone and I saw at a glance that she hadn't replaced her knickers after her exhibition of lovemaking.

"I don't know about you, Victoria, but I'm exhausted," she said. She did indeed look tired. Her hair was wet and straggly, but there was a rosy glow to her face.

"I am quite tired," I admitted. Beatrice jumped on to the bed and knelt beside me.

"Did you enjoy the demonstration?" she asked. I really did not know how to answer. I had watched her pleasure two young Austrian men in turn while our headmistress explained their actions. I blushed as I recalled how excited I had become watching them perform extraordinary acts upon each other.

"Y-yes," I stammered, "it was, uh, exciting."

"That's good. I really wanted to be the one that Madame selected."

"Didn't you mind being watched while you, um, uh..."

"While I fornicated do you mean, Victoria?"

"Uh, yes, I suppose so."

"Well, why not. If you've been trained to do something well, why not show off your skills."

"Do the other girls think the same?"

"Oh yes, I think so. There was quite a competition for tonight's show, but Madame says I'm the best at fellatio, and I do adore having a man lick me really deeply." I blushed again at the memory of Eric kneeling between Bea's legs and lapping at her sex.

"Do you love Eric or Hermann?" I asked innocently.

"Eric's a dear and Hermann has the most wonderful cock. It is so broad that it really stretches you. But you mean love in the sense, am I going to marry them, don't you?"

"Well, yes."

"Of course not, you silly. They're just for training, like the other boys. I'm going to marry a rich man and keep him happy for as long as he lives."

"Who is he?"

"I don't know. I haven't met one yet – but I will."

"Oh. Did you say there are more boys here?"

"There are five, or is it six. No, it's five. Madame employs them around the house but they are really here to help us girls practise the arts of love. Look I'm ready to sleep, can you undo my corset?" She turned her back to me.

"Yes, of course," I started to undo the lacing, "Perhaps you could do the same for me. I've never worn one before."

Soon both of us had pulled off the tight garments and our stockings. Beatrice pulled the bedclothes over herself while she was still naked.

"I can't be bothered with my nightdress. Come and cuddle up with me, Victoria." It was another new thing after a day of surprising events but I did as she said and for the first time in my life felt my body touching that of another, skin to skin.

Lessons began next day and soon I was learning the knowledge and skills necessary to please a man, or at least Madame Thackeray's vision of what men wanted in a wife. I studied art, improved my French and began a course in cookery. In the evening I joined my classmates in the drawing room dressed as we had on the first evening, in white corset, stockings, bloomers and a light dressing gown. For our first lesson Madame told us that if we were to give pleasure to a man then we must know what gives us pleasure. That meant "getting to know ourselves", as she put it. She put up pictures of the female anatomy and got us to recite the names for the various parts of our fannies. Then she explained about the clitoris. I didn't even know it existed before but apparently it is what gives women that wonderful experience of climax. She gave us each a small hand mirror and told us to return to our bedrooms. We were to examine our own sex, find our clitoris and stimulate ourselves until we managed an orgasm. It was the strangest homework I had ever been set.

I sat on the bed with my knickers off, my legs apart, holding the mirror at an angle so I could see what was going on down there with just the oil lamp for illumination. I soon found the hard little knob at the top of my slit which I presumed was the fabled clitoris. I twiddled it and rubbed it. I felt a pleasant sensation but I certainly wasn't experiencing raptures like Beatrice had when Eric licked her. I was getting a bit fed up but then Beatrice came in.

"Oh, you're here, I thought you would be in the lesson with Madame," she said as she slipped off her gown and joined me on the bed, "but, I remember now, you are having your first lesson at getting an orgasm." I blushed and squeezed my legs together. She laughed at my modesty.

"Any luck yet?"

I shook my head.

"It's all in the touch. Look, let me help." She wriggled closer and took the mirror from my hand. Then she caressed the inside of my right thigh.

"Come on, open your legs."

Reluctantly, I parted my thighs a little. Beatrice lifted my knees and pushed them wider apart. I rested my head back on the pillows.

"There's no wonder you had trouble. Your bush is so thick I can barely fight my way through to your little knob. It's time we did something about it." Beatrice leapt off the bed and into the bathroom, leaving me confused. A moment later she returned with a bowl of lather and a fearsome blade – a razor. She knelt between my legs and covered my mound with soapy suds.

"Now keep still." I was too scared to move a muscle. The cold, sharp, blade slid over my most sensitive parts but Bea was so skilled that I felt no nicks. In a very short time she wiped the remaining foam away with a towel and sat back to look at her handiwork. I too looked down between my legs and saw a sight I had never seen. My hair had been reduced to a narrow arrow head pointing at my cleft. My vulva was revealed in its pink, crinkled nakedness.

Beatrice licked the fingers of her right hand. The next moment I felt a spasm of electricity pass through me as her fingers touched the lips of my fanny and slipped inside. I had felt dry but with that one touch I immediately began oozing juices. Beatrice's finger slowly moved up and down. My swelling lips parted and revealed the dark depths of my sex. Then she moved up until she found the little hooded tip. Her fingers circled it and teased it. Each movement, each touch, each new sensation sent shudders of pleasure through me.

"Is this it?" I asked breathlessly.

"Not quite. You'll know." Now she had two hands at work, one massaging my clitoris and the other delving deeper and deeper into my crack. Her fingers worked their way in to my vagina, rhythmically moving in and out. Now I could feel a change occurring inside me. A wave of emotion seemed to start in my toes that set my legs quivering. It entered my stomach and up to my breasts and finally burst through my skull. I clenched my hands and cried out. On and on it continued. I thought I was trapped on a pinnacle of pleasure, but gradually, reluctantly, it faded and passed away. I sobbed and shook. Beatrice gently removed her hands and put the covers over me.

"Now that was an orgasm," she said, smiling.

As the days passed I discovered how to give myself pleasure but never did I match that first explosion of feeling that Beatrice gave me. Our evening lessons moved on however, to consider the male anatomy. I was sitting next to Natalie. She was a petite, French girl with piled ringlets of jet black hair. We had made friends because I was able to speak French quite well while the other girls were German or Italian speakers. Although Natalie was as innocent as me about the art of lovemaking she found our lessons most amusing. She giggled and whispered rude asides to me as Madame described to us the workings of the penis. Then Madame opened a small leather case. We all leaned forward to get a peep at what was inside. There, nestling in padded purple velvet, were three items made of glass. Madame lifted one out and held it up for us to see. It was in the shape of the male member, about six to seven inches long, an average size so Madame said. The others were the same, exact in every detail. They had a flat end so that they could rest on a horizontal surface and stand up proudly.

"This evening, ladies," Madame announced, "your task

21

in pairs, is to take one of these fine dildos to your rooms and practise inserting it in each other. I want you to learn how to accept the object into your bodies and to position yourselves for the greatest satisfaction." I gulped as I looked at the dildos. Only one or two fingers had so far penetrated me and these objects looked so huge. I hesitated but Natalie was eager. She grabbed my hand and pulled me from my seat. She took the first dildo that Madame proffered and dragged me up the stairs to the room that she shared.

Natalie flung off her robe and leapt on to the bed.

"Please help me remove this corset. I cannot follow Madame's instruction with my breath being squeezed out." To be truthful there was little of Natalie to be squeezed as she had the smallest waist I had seen in a girl of seventeen years. I agreed with her as I too found the corset restricting of movement. We took it in turns to divest each other of the garment and then sat side by side with our stockings sliding down our calves. Natalie held the dildo between her palms, warming it. We both looked at it for a moment. Then Natalie jumped up, tugged her bloomers down and handed the dildo to me.

"Come, I will try first. Let us see if it fits." She lay back on the bed and pulled her knees up revealing her sex. I could see at once that she was excited because her lips were swollen and glistening pinkly. I knelt facing her and slowly advanced the tip of the dildo towards her gaping crack. She jerked when it touched her flesh.

"Sorry," I said, withdrawing it.

"Non, the first touch was surprise. Allez." She pulled her knees back further. I took a breath and leant closer. This time she did not flinch as the end of the dildo touched and then passed between her lips. The oval knob slid easily into her and then the shaft disappeared inch by inch. She gasped as I gave it a final push. Now only the flat end was visible surrounded by her engorged labia.

"Oh, oui," she sighed, "I am full. Do you think a man will feel the same?"

"I don't know," I replied, "I cannot imagine any penis being as hard as glass. What do I do now?"

"Make it move, like a man would." I gripped the end of the dildo and slid it out a couple of inches, then pushed it in.

"Yes, yes, faster," Natalie urged. I moved it backwards and forwards. It slid easily with Natalie's secretions lubricating it. I quickly found a rhythm and was soon pounding the dildo into her. She screamed, urging me to ever greater exertions. It seemed to go on and on. I was perspiring profusely and my arm was tiring when she let out a piercing cry.

"Oui, Oui. Aah." She trembled violently then released her thighs at last. I sat back leaving the dildo embedded in her. My arm was tired and stiff.

"I think I will prefer it when the man has to exert himself," I said. Natalie sat up, still panting and pulled the dildo from her vagina.

"Oh but it was worth your effort, my dear. Now it is your turn."

There were no lessons on Saturdays, so most weeks, if the weather was good, we would go out for walks in the mountains. By late October, winter was approaching and already there was snow on the peaks that surrounded us. Natalie and I decided to visit the nearest village to purchase some fresh fruit. We walked down the rough track. The village was poor and there were only a handful of stalls in the market place. The villagers did their best to ignore us. Did they shun us because of what we got up to at the school? Did they even know? Or was it merely distrust of strangers. No one offered us fruit for sale.

There was a boy standing by the last stall. He looked to

be about the same age as us but was quite short and dressed in very rough clothes.

"You want?" He said vaguely and beckoned us to follow him. Thinking that he might know of a store of fruit we heeded him as he hurried up a narrow alley between two buildings. At the rear there was a wooden shack leaning against the stone building. He opened the door and entered. I ducked my head and joined Natalie in the rough shed. Sunlight entered through the many cracks in the walls and roof. The boy turned to face us.

"Me, Albert," he said, "You get me job at school?" With that he lifted up his torn and grubby smock and revealed a huge penis. I gasped and covered my mouth with my gloved hand. Natalie giggled. Albert gripped his member with his right hand but he could barely reach around it. He waggled it at us. The pink glans sparkled in the sunlight.

"You want?" He waved his immense cock at each of us.

"No, no, put it away," I insisted and waved him away. He let the hem of his smock fall, but now that he was fully excited, it did little to hide it. Natalie began to question him and through a mixture of broken English and poorly interpreted German we gathered that he was an orphan, completely destitute and without any means of support now that he was passed sixteen years of age. We agreed to pass on his request to Madame Thackeray and said that he should present himself at the school on Monday.

That evening I waited for Bea to return to tell her about Albert and ask her advice. It was gone midnight when she returned. A look of surprise greeted me.

"You are still awake, Victoria. I was sure you would be asleep at this time." She climbed gingerly onto the bed and lay face down.

"What is the matter, Bea? Where have you been? Are you ill?"

"I'll be all right, Victoria, don't worry. I have been

24

having an extra lesson with Madame Hulot."

"What kind of lesson?" I asked innocently.

"What do you think? Lessons in what men like from a woman. There is much more to learn in the second year, my dear."

"More than we saw you do on that first evening?"

Beatrice turned her head towards me and gave me a thin smile. "Far more. Now we are learning the dark arts of lovemaking. Look." She pulled up her gown, which I noted was now black lace. Underneath was a black satin corset but her buttocks were bare. I was astonished to see that both white globes were criss-crossed with red marks.

"Madame Hulot did that? Had you done something wrong?"

"Not at all, I performed perfectly." There was a pride in her voice. "She held me down over her lap while Eric wielded the cane. I cried, but did not struggle. Then with Madame Hulot pressing down on my shoulders he knelt behind me. I thought he was going to enter me from behind but he forced his way into my forbidden passage." I had no idea what she was talking about. "But forget what I have told you, they are secrets for your next year of tuition. Why are you not asleep?"

I told her about Albert, his desire for a job and his immense attribute. Bea agreed to put the matter to the Principal and then bade me to put the light out and get to sleep.

A few evenings later the six of us were sitting in pairs in the drawing room with the candelabra and oil lamps fully lit. Madame placed the three glass dildos in their padded box and said.

"I think that is enough of the artificial. Now for the real thing." She clapped her hand and immediately the door opened. Three young men entered wearing knee length smoking jackets. At the front were Wilhelm and Heinrich who worked in the yard, chopping wood and stoking the fires in the kitchen. Behind them was Albert. Albert saw Natalie and me and immediately came and stood in front of us. The other two boys went and stood in front of our classmates.

"Welcome, gentlemen," Madame said, "now you may disrobe." The three boys flung off their jackets. All six of us girls gasped at the sight of three naked men. Albert's body was completely white except for his arms and lower legs, and he looked and smelt a lot cleaner than when we had last seen him. What had not changed, however, was his long, thick penis. It was considerably bigger than the glass dildo. It stood out proudly, quivering slightly, its root buried in a mass of brown curls, with a fist-sized sac dangling below.

"Now girls, you may caress the shaft and lightly touch the glans." Natalie leaned closer and reached out a hand. Albert was staring down at the two cherries in the centre of the small moons that rested on the white satin of her corset. She placed a finger on the shaft about halfway along its length and slid it first one way then the other. Albert groaned and at once a fountain of milky fluid burst from the tip of his cock and hit Natalie between her breasts. She recoiled with a cry and fell backwards. Madame strode over to see what disaster had occurred.

"Really, Albert, I must teach you some measure of control." Albert looked as unhappy and embarrassed as he possibly could. His penis had shrunk to a quarter of its erect size and hung limply and forlorn. "You must restore it quickly, Albert. You are young and should not need to waste time." Madame whispered kindly to him and leant down to take his penis in her hands. She massaged and caressed it and in but a minute or two it began to swell and stiffen once again. Madame turned to me.

"Now, Victoria. You feel it. I am sure we will have no

26

more intemperate accidents." Albert took a step towards me and I slid off the chair to kneel in front of him. Now his penis was at the level of my breasts. Albert looked down at them, his eyes wide with the delight of seeing my full bosoms exposed above my corset. I saw his penis stiffen and rise another inch or so, beckoning to be fondled. The foreskin had pulled back completely revealing the door-knob-sized glans pierced by a small hole which now gaped open. I placed the palm of my right hand on his abdomen, lowered my fingers into the shrub of pubic hair and then bending my wrist, slid my fingers slowly and gently along his shaft. My thumb rubbed along the underside feeling the tight, smooth skin. When I got to the point where the pink glans began I stopped and squeezed gently. Albert moaned softly. I looked up into his face and could see his eyes wobbling in their sockets. His knees started to buckle.

"I think you had better lie down, Albert," I said quietly. He needed no second bidding and he subsided to the floor, soon lying flat on his back with his legs apart on either side of my knees. I had not let go of his penis and now with it pointing towards the ceiling I began to massage it up and down. The skin moved easily. On each down-stroke, the skin of the glans was pulled taut so that it glistened with the reflected light of the candles. On the up stroke, the foreskin slid over the tip. Albert groaned with pleasure on each movement. I was so intent on my actions that I found myself becoming excited as well. I slipped my left hand into my bloomers. Already my pubis felt hot and moist and I found my little knob hard and erect. I rubbed it in time with the vibrations of my right hand on Albert's cock.

"Harder, harder," Albert muttered between gasps of pleasure. I increased my frequency of movement, both hands working hard, the right on Albert and the left on myself. I began to wonder if Albert could be brought to orgasm so soon after spraying Natalie with his semen. I need not have feared however, for just as my arm began to ache, Albert stretched out his legs and arched his back, and another fountain of white fluid shot from his penis. The shock pushed me to the point of orgasm too. The spasms of pleasure made me cry.

"Oh, bravo," cheered Natalie clapping her hands gleefully, "You have done him for sure, and yourself too." I sat back on my heels, holding my hands up in front of me and stretching out the fingers to relieve the stiffness of the exertion. Albert lay on his back, panting.

"Very good, Victoria." I hadn't realised that Madame had been standing nearby watching me perform, "but you must learn that when you are servicing a man, his pleasure is paramount and you should not divide your energy by pleasing yourself as well as him. You will go to my office and wait for me to come and teach you some lessons in the etiquette of lovemaking. Now Natalie your turn to work on Albert."

I rose to my feet, and turned towards the door. I was upset that I had apparently transgressed and earned Madame's displeasure. What punishment had she prepared for me?

BBBW
by Landon Dixon

Tom was just doing his job, cleaning Dr Klinghoffer's office, when Zelda Zeist blew in.

"Sorry I'm late, Doctor!" she gushed, pulling off her coat, flinging aside her purse, and flopping down on the psychologist's brown leather couch.

Tom tried to get a word in edgewise, any other wise, to explain to the chattering woman that he wasn't the esteemed Dr Klinghoffer – just a lowly member of the building cleaning crew. But Zelda, obviously on her first session with the good Doctor (since she didn't recognise Tom for who he wasn't), was hearing none of it, nattering non-stop about her problems, shortcomings, and neuroses. She went on and on down the endless list, a headshrinker's wet dream.

Tom was having some wide-awake wet dreams of his own, too. And they had nothing to do with Sigmund Freud, or his mother. Because what he was looking at and into wasn't the babbling woman's mind; it was her chest.

Even flat on her back, Zelda's breasts bulged out her too-tight sweater like twin water balloons under Saran Wrap. She was obviously braless, the free-range boobs jumping all over the place, jumbling around in rhythm to her increasingly hysterical gesticulations. They splayed, they flopped, they shivered – together and separately; they

29

were pushed together and up, towards the heavens, as the woman ranted about her fears and phobias, more 'issues' than the backorder catalogue of a sex magazine.

Tom, an amiable schlub whose only fault was a burning lack of ambition, understood little of what the well-endowed woman was saying (he wasn't really listening), but everything of what her ill-packaged tits were telling him. Because his two true passions in life were boobs (the bigger the better) and the women blessed to possess them.

No one had studied more pictures and video of naked female breasts than Tom. Short and chubby, with a greying goatee and balding head, he could certainly pass for a certified doctor of psychology. But his specialty was actually the physiology of big boobs, and the very special psychology of the babes attached to them.

And as he observed Zelda's jostling hooters, with something less than clinical detachment, he made an instant and important diagnosis. "Stand up," he said.

Zelda zipped her lips for the first time since she'd stormed into the book-lined office. "Stand up?" she asked, parting them again.

"Yes, stand." Tom's voice carried an air of authority that his high school diploma couldn't hope to back up.

Zelda struggled to get off the couch. Tom helped her, his knowing, undressing eyes locked on the woman's shuddering tits.

They managed to get her and her precious chest cargo vertical, and Tom got a real good look at both. She was short and slightly chunky, her long, brown hair a mess, her voluptuous figure done no justice by the ratty, too-small sweater and baggy pair of army pants she was wearing. She had sparkling green eyes and a full, sensuous mouth, however, an adorable moon-face. And those large, hanging boobs.

"Why don't you wear a bra?" Tom asked frankly.

"Why don't I ...? Well, um, I–"

"You're aware of the mid-arm rule, are you not?"

"The ... huh?"

Tom shook his head, stroked his goatee, studying Zelda's breasts like a savvy shopper studies the plump chickens hanging in a kosher butcher's window. "A woman's breasts should dangle no lower than the mid-point of her upper arm when she's standing – fully-clothed. Now, there're certain concessions for the busty, of course. But still, a properly-fitting bra is essential to the proper packaging and presentation of one's breasts. To properly lift and shape and support. And show off. Remove your sweater, please."

Zelda's eyes widened. "Remove my ...? Hey, I came here to have my head examined, Doctor, not my body."

Tom dismissed her comment with a brusque wave of his hand, really getting into his role. Here was a chance for someone other than himself to actually benefit from his voluminous knowledge of the physical and psychological aspects of big boobery. "All your problems are trivial compared to your tits," he stated with absolute conviction. "Your breasts are the issue – the way you handle them, exhibit them, treat them. They're the eight-hundred-pound elephants in the room, my dear. Now, sweater off. Let me see."

Zelda gave her head a shake. But he *was* the doctor, and they *were* obsessed with all things sexual, weren't they? So, she shrugged her shoulders and tried to peel off her stretch-wrapped sweater. But it got stuck under her overhanging breasts.

Tom helped her fight the skin-tight garment, until at last they succeeded in rolling it up over her chest. And her bountiful boobs tumbled free.

Tom took a step back, getting perspective, getting a raging hard-on at the naked eye-view of Zelda's breasts, swimming around on her chest as she wrestled the sweater over her head. The pale, smooth-skinned melons sported coral-pink areolas wide enough to span a man's open mouth, cotton-candy pink nipples both thick and jutting.

Tom nodded his head, pronounced his diagnosis. "You suffer from breast denial."

Zelda dropped her misshapen sweater onto the couch. "Breast denial?"

"Yes." Tom stepped forward and boldly clutched the ponderously swaying bottoms of the woman's breasts.

She gasped, as he hefted and squeezed, weighed.

"You're a ... triple-D," he shrewdly assessed, raising an eyebrow along with his cock as he felt up the soft, silky skin. "Forty ... two inches around."

He abruptly dropped her tits, causing her to rock forward. "You have overly-large breasts and yet you dress and act like you're a normal-breasted woman," he lectured, his hands still tingling with the heated lingering feel of her boobs, her boobs still tingling with the heated lingering feel of his hands. "No bra, a sweater too small, talking over your tits, wilfully ignoring them and their gravity, their influence on the world all around you. A classic case of breast denial."

He stroked his chin more rapidly this time, his chin now a symbolic phallic replacement for his dick, which was one pulse away from busting loose the zipper on his jeans. "Most big-boobed women suffer from some degree of breast denial. They don't want to admit they're a double-D, or triple-H. It's a very common discontent." He paused dramatically, eyes glued to Zelda's bared breasts. "And, dare I say, the root cause of all of your problems."

"Breast denial? Really?" Zelda gulped.

"Look no further than your chest, my dear," Tom counselled sagely. "As I don't."

"But-but what can I do?"

32

Tom grasped the woman's jugs again, this time shoving them right up into her startled face. "Acknowledge them!" he asserted. "Admit their well-above-average size and scope, their impressive weight and girth. By God, don't diminish them! They're not normal, you're not normal, and that's a good thing – two good things."

Zelda staggered back under the weight of the revelation, the man's fingers digging deep into her meaty tit-flesh as he dug deep into her psyche. She hit the wall, jarring a paper degree loose and sending it plummeting to the carpet.

Tom openly groped Zelda's breasts, with the fanatical fervour of the closet boobologist, working his fingers up onto her protruding nipples and dialling them in like he was dialling in the source of all her angst. "You're a BBBW – a big-boobed beautiful woman – and there's nothing wrong with that. In fact, there's everything right with that. But you have to admit it, embrace it, enhance it!"

Zelda stared over her breasts at the over-excited man, her face flushed, her chest thick with a sensuous, tingling heat. "I'm a ..."

"You're a big-boobed beautiful woman!" Tom shouted.

His hot breath steamed into her face and her breasts, his hot, sweaty hands luxuriating in the baby's bottom feel, the unreal heaviness of her magnificent mams. He pushed his body against hers, his jeaned hard-on into her panted pussy, working her tits with every fibre of his being. He pinched her rubbery nipples and rolled them, his lips bare inches away from capturing and sucking on them.

She undulated against the wall, the man, her eyelids fluttering and breasts shuddering. Her chest was on fire like never before, waves of white-hot pleasure rolling through her overheated body from where his hands mauled her brimming breast-meat, his fingers tugged on her buzzing breast-tips.

"I'm a ... big-boobed beautiful woman!" Zelda gasped,

staring fiercely into Tom's fiery eyes, burning with confidence and eroticism. The weight of all her foolish problems had been lifted from her shoulders, like he was lifting her breasts.

"Good," Tom remarked. He dropped the dripping woman's shimmering tits, pulled back. "My prescribed treatment is a bra intervention. And here's your prescription."

He handed her a hundred-dollar gift certificate to Rackers, a downtown lingerie store and brassiereum.

Zelda insisted that Tom accompany her on her tit-fitting trip to Rackers. Still in the character of Dr Klinghoffer, he commented that it was most unusual for a psychologist to accompany one of his patients on an outing, but in her case, he'd make an exception. Due to her two outstanding exceptions, he failed to articulate.

They met outside the brassiere and lingerie retailer the following afternoon. Zelda was wearing a slightly roomier top this time – a white satin blouse with ivory buttons that still strained to hold her back. And she was wearing a bra. Only, it was totally inadequate for the enormous job, far too small and weak to handle the hefty loads. Her boobs spilled out the tops and sides and bottoms, cups overflowing everywhere, stretched-taut straps biting into her shoulders and back.

Tom surveyed her billowing chest, her prominent nipples almost piercing the thin garments she wore. He shook his head and stroked his goatee, tut-tutting. He was turned-on, certainly, adopting a wide-legged stance in an effort to hide his erection, but he was still concerned.

"It's no wonder you're so down on the world," he postulated, placing a hand on a hooter, "when you're hurting so up top. Rest assured, the ladies at Rackers will measure, plumb, weigh, fit, calibrate, and select a series of bras that will put a smile on your face and a rainbow in your mind. You'll feel and look ten years younger, twenty pounds lighter. Snug and secure, packaged properly for projection, you'll be able to face the world chest-on, cool and confident and big-boobed proud."

Zelda grinned, held up a pair of crossed fingers. Then she entered the women's-only shop.

Tom pressed his nose to the tinted glass. He shielded out the sun and squinted, eyeballing the racks and racks of cotton, satin, lace, leather, and spandex-lycra bras, in all shapes, sizes, and colours. And only when his mobile phone went off, forcing him to peel his drool-fastened lips from the window, did he realise how much time had passed.

It was Zelda. "I'm all fitted!" she gushed. "Finally fitted correctly and comfortably. But now I have to choose some bras to buy – and I need your help."

It was highly unorthodox – had he been an actual doctor – to get so involved with the woman. But as Tom, unlicensed boobologist, it was a natural. He and his cock sprang into action.

He checked out the clerks through the glass. And when they were otherwise occupied, he darted inside the store, ducked in behind a bra rack. He poked his head up, spotted Zelda chatting with a clerk at the rear of the shop, near the changing rooms. He flashed her a series of hand-signals that would've done a Delta Force commando proud, then stealthily approached, loading up on new bra smell, feeling up sensually-crafted cups every step of the way. Before finally charging into a vacant changing room.

She joined him seconds later, her arms loaded with bras. She spilled them onto a bench and quickly undid her blouse, unfastened her own woeful bra. Her breasts exploded out into the open, an avalanche of pink-capped snowcones.

Tom sucked air into his lungs, his internal temperature and the temperature in the suddenly-cramped changing room soaring. He reached out and touched Zelda's tits.

"Oh!" she yelped, arching her back.

He gently caressed the woman's rising and falling boobs with the twitching tips of his fingers, no longer a phoney doctor, just a real man. Their eyes met, and it was clear she saw him for what he was, and loved him for it.

"Is everything all right in there?" the clerk called from outside.

"Yes-yes!" Zelda exhaled. "More than all right." She smiled at Tom, clutching his hands to her heaving breasts. "I've never been more right. Hand me a triple-D, size 42 bra, will you, 'doctor'?"

There were all kinds of brassieres – halter bras and balconette bras and strapless bras and plunge bras; full cups and demi-cups, soft cups, moulded cups; white, black, red, blue, purple, and pink brassieres; lacy and sheer, see-through, nipple-baring bras for boudoir teasing and titillation; solid, satiny, nipple-hiding bras for board meetings and family dinners. Bras for all seasons and all reasons. The only things they shared in common were cups you could serve breakfast cereal in, not an inch of padding to be found anywhere.

Tom handed them to Zelda, along with his personal and professional comments as an over-the-shoulder-boulder-holder connoisseur. And Zelda slung them on and clasped them together, using more of Tom's hands-on help. So that by the time they finally got down to the last brassiere, the only thing harder than Zelda's new-found resolve, was Tom's zipper-splitting cock.

Zelda gazed at herself in the mirror, as Tom lovingly fitted the strapless black lace demi-cup over her breasts, hefted and hooked her up securely in the back. They both marvelled at how the reinforced bra blossomed out her tits in a most enticing Elizabethan manner. The rounded tops of her form-fitted boobs jiggled delightfully when she giggled, the snow-white flesh piled up high and deep enough to blissfully suffocate any full-grown man.

Zelda spun around, into Tom's arms. "How can I ever repay you for all of your help – your wise counsel?" she breathed. "I feel like a new woman." She started to cry.

He stared down at her bumpers, his breath caught in his throat by the awesome pressure of her boobs against his chest. "My pleasure," he squeaked, meaning every word of it.

She flung her arms around him and kissed him on the lips.

Their mouths melted together. They kissed hungrily, ferociously. Zelda flashed her tongue into his mouth, tangling it with the silver tongue that had set her free. Tom grasped the sides of Zelda's lace-contained breasts, squeezing the thick flesh through the thin, but strong and sensuous, bra-material.

She groaned, and he broke away from her mouth. He dropped his head lower, started raining kisses down on the soft, pudding-propped-up tops of her boobs. She moaned her encouragement.

He got a firmer grip on her cups and heaved them up and down, kissing, licking the rippling tit-flesh over and over. He sunk his teeth into the rich, vanilla-jello confection, leaving slick, red bite marks behind on her ivory skin. Then he dropped his head even lower and tongued her ripe nipples through the sexy bra.

"Oh, god, yes!" Zelda cried, trembling in Tom's hands. This was truly therapy of the very best kind.

Tom lapped at one swollen nipple and then the other, clotting the bra lace with his saliva, teasing Zelda's half-inchers longer and harder yet. He licked and sucked on her nipples, painted her blazing areolas with his eager tongue, all the while squeezing and kneading her barely, but securely, containerized boobs. Until, with a Herculean

37

strength borne of sexual desperation, he shovelled her tits together and bit into both of her nipples at once.

She screamed her joy, the world outside the thin partition of the changing room completely forgotten. She beat her fists on Tom's shoulders, lungs bellowing in his hands.

He knew it was time for one final positive reinforcement. So he pushed Zelda down to her knees and pulled out his cock and plunged it into her cleavage, dick-stick style. The straight-down titty-fuck. No up-and-under that even a small-breasted woman could handle to some extent. This was the sheer mountain-face tit-plunge that only the well-developed ladies could truly handle. And Zelda handled it easily.

She spat on Tom's cock, into her cleavage, greasing the dick-defying action. He crowded her face and chest, riding her boobs, pushing balls-down into her tit-tunnel. The super-tight, superheated sensation enveloped his throbbing shaft and reverberated all through his quivering body. He bent at the knees, lifted back up again, pumping his prick in between Zelda's bared breasts, the wet-hot friction incredible. As she licked at his stomach, swirled her tongue around in his bellybutton.

"Fuck my tits!" she hissed, folding her arms under her bulging bra for even more support, a big-boobed beautiful woman in breast denial no more.

Sweat poured off Tom's face and his knees cracked as he scissored up and down. His bent-arrow cock surged back and forth in Zelda's breastworks, plugging her vice-like cleavage. He squatted like crazy, gaping down at her, until the wicked 180-degree sights and sounds and sensations became too much for him. "Fuck, I'm gonna come!" he grunted, head spinning and balls boiling.

"Come in between my boobs! My great big beautiful boobs!" Zelda wailed, sandwiching her tits together.

Tom furiously spelunked her stifling chest-canyon one last time, and then his cock exploded, rocking him back on his heels. Jet after jet of sizzling semen blasted out of his cap and into Zelda's cleavage, soaking her breasts and bra; blowing his mind and thrilling his body.

While he could still be counted on to be there whenever Zelda needed to 'unburden' herself, Tom now actively sought out other big-boobed women living in breast denial. He dispensed advice and glad-tidings, hands-on and open-mouthed, helping the BBBW's realise what they had and how they should best handle them, for the benefit of all.

The unambitious tit-man had finally found his true calling in life. And he embraced it with a passion.

Snooty Pussy
by Fransiska Sherwood

Maria was sitting at her desk, drenched in a pool of ghostly white light. Chestnut curls tumbled into her face from a loose knot piled on her head she'd haphazardly secured with a pencil. Her glasses were two half-moons that perched on the end of her nose and signalled, if anyone had been there to disturb her, 'Go away, I'm studying'.

At least that's what she was supposed to be doing. But she couldn't concentrate.

She'd been reading a textbook on the Italian Renaissance. Her essay had got to be on her tutor's table the next morning. But long ago her eyes had drifted from the text to the pictures, and already she was flicking idly through the pages.

At Michelangelo's David, she halted.

The white marble gleamed under the halogen light, and his body seemed to lift itself off the page.

Had the flashlights caught the crystalline glint of the marble? Or was it just an optical illusion created by the darker background? Perhaps it was the desk lamp?—doing the same thing to the white that strobe lights did in a disco. But there was nothing purply about him. He was pure, radiant whiteness. God-like, ethereal. The embodiment of classical perfection.

Yet Maria wasn't impressed.

She scanned David's body. Was he really a perfect example of manhood, a flawless piece of art? Near divine? He didn't fulfil all her criteria. His hands seemed too big. Disproportionate. Her eyes were always drawn to the arm hanging by his side, the hand so near to that other item of interest. And if his hand was too large, then his cock was too small. Or, let's say, these days a girl prefers something bigger.

She knew, of course, Michelangelo was drawing on a much older tradition, where the giant phallus was an object of ridicule. Saved for fawns and centaurs and scenes of bacchanal copulation on red/black vases and terracotta oil lamps. The essence of male beauty was a small penis that nestled among opulent curls like a new-born kitten, licked smooth by its mother's tongue. So David was endowed with a rather shrivelled specimen.

How tastes change.

She retrieved the pencil and shook her hair free. A spiralling cascade of ringlets. Michelangelo's idea of a beautiful youth he may be. But not what she'd call drop-dead gorgeous. He wouldn't turn *her* head on the street. Didn't his cheeks still have a bit too much puppy-fat? And wasn't the cap of curls he wore far too heavy-looking? Even if she imagined his hair to be dark brown, soft and springy, scented with rich Mediterranean oils, she wouldn't have been prompted to run her fingers through it, the way she was now doing with her own.

Her thoughts were interrupted by the purr of an engine. The yellow beam of a headlight sliced through the darkness in the courtyard below. Maria bowed her head. Tried to look as if she were engrossed in her studies. She knew who'd just arrived.

It really was time she got some curtains put up. Stuck up there at the window she now felt rather vulnerable. Like realising someone can see into your shower.

42

A few minutes later she heard the door to the flat below her bang shut. Yes, Tom was home. Her leather-clad neighbour. If you followed him out, you could smell him. That special tang of rawhide that lingers in the air. The way the smell of the saddle clings to jodhpurs. When he wasn't in leather, he wore a tattered denim jacket, tattooed in biro with the names of rock bands. On the back of it was an appliquéd tiger, its teeth bared fang-like.

It didn't scare Maria one little bit.

The low throb of his music began to seep through the floor. The walls to the place were so thin she had a good idea of all his comings and goings and doings. Tonight he was alone. At least she'd not have to suffer the silly giggling of some dumb chick he'd picked up. Or later their moans and groans. Only the dull thudding base of his stereo that pulsed through her body as she lay in bed. Until her heart and lungs and womb resonated with its beat.

And she'd thought having her own flat was going to be better than sharing a room in some student hostel.

He was one of the few people in the building she knew at all. And she'd decided early on he was not her *niveau*. A be-leathered biker with a mane of yellow hair. He was primitive, an animal, and oozed with the confidence it was worth being the prey he stalked. But Maria made her own conquests. And he wasn't worth the quarry.

They'd never spoken. On the few occasions they'd met on the stairs, they'd skirted round each other. Eyes warily looking the other over.

The next morning Maria was woken by the low growl of a tiger prowling the undergrowth of her subconscious. Only gradually did she realise, as her eyes fluttered open, that the sound was her neighbour roaring off to wherever he went. She drifted between waking and sleeping, side-tracked by images of the big cats. Beautiful, dangerous creatures that stalked about in her mind for a few moments before she

43

shook them off, yawned, stretched and rolled over to look at the time on the alarm clock.

Oh no! She was going to be late, and that essay was only half finished. Well, he was just going to have to wait for it, wasn't he.

As she wandered about half-dressed, she began to wonder what exactly Tom could see from below. Had the far side of the courtyard been anything other than a blank wall, she'd have had curtains put up much earlier. She'd thought she was only on view sitting at her desk. But could he see in from down there? And what had he seen? Had he watched her undress, perhaps? A shiver ran through her, a contrary mixture of shock and excitement.

But he couldn't be interested in Maria. Judging by what he brought home, he preferred blondes. Brassy bottle jobs, with big tits squeezed into black leathers. Cheap and tacky. And she certainly didn't fit that mould.

Maria was dark and exotic, her Italian ancestry plain to see in her olive skin, deep hazelnut eyes, the mass of dark brown curls and long black lashes. Not his taste at all.

Or was he intrigued by her dark looks? Did he perhaps want to find out what kind of passions smouldered beneath the haughty disdain? Or had he already given up on a bad job? After that one time they'd met at the letterboxes and she'd ignored his 'hello'.

It was a pity if he had. She would have loved to take a proper look at him, study those wild, rugged features—so unlike the immobile, sculpted contours of art. There was something tantalising about that feline grin, the twinkle in those pale brown eyes, the way a beard just bristled through his chin. But how to get near him when they didn't even speak? And the last thing she wanted to do was encourage him.

Did he even look up when he parked his bike? Maria didn't know. But if he did, what kind of impression did she

44

make on him, sitting in the window? Did she just look sober and studious with a pair of reading glasses perched on the end of her nose? Or did she remind him of the timid secretary in comedy sketches who takes off her glasses, lets down her hair, and turns into a vamp.

An idea much more to her liking.

She wandered over to the mirror, and heaped her hair onto the top of her head in a jumble of wayward curls. Short tendrils framed the nape of her neck and S-shaped strands fell into her face. She did a Marilyn Monroe pout at herself in the mirror.

Mmm, not bad.

She ran a critical eye over the rest of her body. If 'History of Art' turned out to be a flop, she could always take up modelling.

Her best feature were her legs: lean and seemingly endless, the skin always a honeyed tan. She had great feet, too. Narrow and straight, with long toes like a statue. They looked good in elegant shoes and strappy sandals. But who was interested in feet? Her hips were slim—she smoothed over them—and her stomach flat and taut. The ideal figure for the beaches of Rimini. Guaranteed to make other women curl with envy. She was classy, racy—and even wearing jeans and a floppy jumper she had style.

Maria smiled. Had she just caught herself indulging in a bit of vanity? What if she had, it was hardly a sin. Nothing she need fear retribution for.

She cupped her hands around her breasts, clad in a seductive, dark blue bra, and allowed her hair to tumble into her face. Like two russet apples the perfect rounds nestled in the lacy cups, her skin as smooth as chamois.

What would Tom think if he could see her now? Would he like what he saw? Or was the sight of her half-dressed nothing new? Had he come back one night and she'd unwittingly given him a strip-tease show? Had he since

45

been slipping out into the darkness every night, hungry for more? A peeping Tom. Now, in her books, that was a sin.

And didn't she like the idea.

Slowly she unhooked her bra, slipped the straps from her shoulders and let it drop to the ground, her eyes trained on her performance in the mirror. Did he like midnight blue underwear? Wasn't it sexier than black? A little thrill of excitement rippled through her body and she felt her nipples tighten and her skin break out in goose pimples.

Had she given him a good show? Well, this time there was more to come.

She began to wriggle out of her panties. Not as easy to do with as much effect or conviction. That part of her routine needed more practice. Maybe different underwear? She pulled a pair of shell-pink cami-knickers out of a drawer. The colour went so well with her olive skin, showing it off even better than white. As she slipped into them, the silky fabric caressed her cheeks like the whispered breath of a lover and sent a tingle right through her.

She turned to see the back view in the mirror, her bottom poking out behind her. She arched her back some more, leant forward to catch her breast in side profile. At this angle it flopped quite voluptuously before her. Maria couldn't resist closing her hand round it, and giving a little squeeze. Lying on your back rendered you almost flat-chested, she realised—from now on she'd better make sure she was always on top, taking full advantage of gravity.

On top was where she always wanted to be, anyway. In more senses than one.

She lifted the lacy hem of the cami-knickers to reveal a bit more bottom. Then ran her finger over the skin, just underneath the fabric. Wouldn't Tom like to do that? Trace a line right to the triangle of silk between her legs that concealed her sex, already pulsating with a wanton desire.

46

Or maybe he preferred something more theatrical?

She hunted through her drawers for a chiffon scarf and then danced in front of the mirror, draping it over her shoulders and trailing it over her breasts like a feather boa. The scarf tickled, making the goose pimples break out all over her once more. Brown and prominent, her nipples now stood to attention, offering themselves to the material caress. She pulled the scarf across them, first lightly, then with ever more friction, backwards and forwards until the peaks became hot and sore and the muscles of her cervix contracted, caught in a mild cramp.

She let the scarf fall to the floor, clasped each breast and squeezed, imagining the hard, burning hands of a man on her flesh. Then she let her nipples escape through a crack between her fingers, before clamping the berry-hard points between them. A pinching that made them greedy for more. She wished she could suck them. Or even better—someone would come and do it for her. Right this minute.

Little spasms were now shooting through the ring of muscle at the entrance to her sex. Her hands left her breasts and swept down over her hips while she swayed about in front of the mirror. Then one hand stole over the springy mound of hair hidden beneath the pink silk and began to gently rub her clitoris through the shimmering material.

There was no harm in pretending her fingers were his, was there?

The material was soon glistening with her own juices. Maria played with the sensation for a moment or two, then whisked the cami-knickers to the floor.

Had Tiger Tom already seen the dark crop of curls that adorned her pubis? Did he want to wind the hair round his finger like she was now doing? Stroke and caress her flesh?

The spasms inside her were becoming ever more impatient. Maria knew she'd now gone beyond a game. She needed more stimulation than merely imagining her fingers

47

were someone else's. As pleasurable as it was.

She picked up the scarf, threaded it between her legs and began to pull it back and forth, rubbing her clitoris, the lips of her vulva, the tight ring of muscle at her anus with the chiffon. Delicious friction that soon left the material wet and slick, oiling her parts with frenzied strokes.

Then she crouched before the mirror, her legs wide open, so that she could see what she was doing and could saw deeper between the palpitating folds of flesh. She was ready to come. She knew it wouldn't take much more. She dropped the scarf and traced mad little circles round the opening to her sex before inserting her finger into the aching hole. She knew the spot she was looking for. A few rapid motions and waves of pleasure radiated through her stomach.

She staggered backwards onto the bed, dizzy from crouching and the physical sensation. There she stayed, reliving the experience again and again until she was so weak with exertion she could come no more.

She got up again at around ten and showered. She felt wicked, sullied, but nevertheless pleased with herself. Not only had she broken the ultimate taboo, so carefully instilled by her Catholic upbringing, but she'd missed her tutorial. Not that it was the first time she'd done what she'd been told she mustn't, but this time it had been a veritable orgy. She wished, though, the love lavished on her by a series of imagined lovers had been real. There had to be someone out there who could make her feel that good, make her come a thousand times over. She was fed up with waiting for that knight in silver armour to arrive on his jet-black charger.

So how about a knight in jet-black leather on a gleaming silver charger?

Maybe something animal was what she'd been looking for all along. Someone who knew nothing of the refinements of art. A man more interested in the physical, with a primitive, dirty streak.

New prospects suddenly opened up before her. What games they could play with his rumbling bass strumming though her body, or clad in the raw scent of leather. Or on top of that bike at midnight, even. Out there in the courtyard. Stark naked. For everyone to see.

Now that would be a sin worth suffering retribution for.

City Of Melbourne
by Eva Hore

Landing this job in Melbourne had been a dream of mine for years. I work for a big company in the States and over the last ten years they've opened offices all over the world. I'd been lucky enough to have been transferred to Tokyo, London, Madrid and now here. The only problem was that I was so busy working I didn't have time to go out and socialise.

One night last week while I was working late I noticed some activities going on in an office building across from me in Collins Street. A woman and man seemed to be arguing. By their body language it was quite heated. Suddenly, the guy pushed her back into her chair and stormed out.

She appeared to be crying. Intrigued, I watched as she lifted the phone, spoke into it briefly, and then hung up. She rose, left the office to go into an adjoining room, leaving me to wonder whether to continue watching or finish up with my work. The decision was made when she re-entered a while later wearing what looked like a skin-tight leather outfit and carrying a box.

My interest was now really piqued, but I was unable to see what she was doing clearly. I remembered in one of the associate partner's office that I'd seen a telescope. As no one was about I hurried in and returned as quickly as

51

possible. I closed the door hoping not to be disturbed. The last thing I needed was to be reported as a *peeping tom*.

Adjusting the focus lens I zoomed in. Wow, this woman was hot and her outfit was dynamite. Her enormously large breasts spilled over the top of a leather vest she was nearly wearing. She had on leather hot pants and thigh high boots. Her long, blonde hair hung halfway down her back, cascading into curls and her face was exquisite. Large eyes, upturned nose and red painted, pouting lips.

She was rummaging around in a box and I saw her remove some handcuffs and a few other things too small for me to identify. She laid them with a whip across the desk and then she was turning around, her back to me as she sashayed over to the door.

I held my breath wondering who would be there. A mousey-looking woman, wearing glasses, a twin-set and plaid skirt entered, carrying some books. She had her head down, her hair pulled back severely off her face, as she shuffled in, in a hunched-over way, giving her the appearance of someone shy and withdrawn. She placed the books on the desk and was on her way out of the door when the woman in black grabbed her by the arm and yanked her back in.

Fuck, I thought. What the hell was going on? I quickly grabbed my chair and scooted back over to the window. I didn't want to miss a thing. They struggled a bit and then the woman in black pushed her up against the wall. She grabbed the handcuffs, snapped them over her wrists and then tied a rope to them.

Climbing up on a chair she looped the rope through some sort of hook and then hoisted her up, tying the end tightly to a railing, when she had her at the right height. Slapping the whip in her hand she paced the floor, then stopped directly in front of her.

She tore the woman's glasses off and threw them across

the room, then lay the whip against her face, slowly running it down to her lips where it lingered over her mouth. It looked as though she wanted her to suck on it but the woman moved her head from side to side. The woman in black threw her head back and appeared to be laughing.

She thrust her hand between the woman's thighs and they stared hard at each other. With one hand still there the other lifted her skirt and I could see she was wearing white panties. She fiddled around for a while and the skirt fell to the floor.

Her hands pushed up the twin set, right over her bra. She had a matronly-looking white bra on and from what I could see her breasts were magnificent, full, with a plunging cleavage. She pulled her bra up over her breasts and they fell heavily into the woman's hands where she crushed them cruelly.

She stood back, allowing me an eyeful, before yanking at her panties to tear them straight off her body. My God, this mousey woman was hairless. I raised the telescope and looked into her face. Her hair had come undone and it hung about her shoulders. There was nothing plain about her now. She was gorgeous, her eyes wild with lust, her mouth open and by the way her chest was heaving I'd say she was clearly enjoying herself.

The blonde picked something off the table and I saw it was a pair of scissors. She pulled her clothing outwards and cut jaggedly through the twin-set before snipping through her bra. The garments hung half over her breasts and under her arms. She looked so fucking sexy I can tell you, tied up and vulnerable. I wanted nothing more than to go over there and join in, suck on those breasts and finger that hairless cunt.

The woman in black again went over to the door. It opened and a guy in a business suit lingered there for a moment. He pulled something out of his pocket, money I think, and she shoved it into her bra. He entered and the woman who was tied up began to struggle against the restraints.

I could feel the distinct throbbing of my cock and shifted uncomfortably in my chair. The guy was old and lecherous-looking. I wanted to somehow save her from him. He strolled around her, touching her breasts, toying with her nipples, while she tried to move away from him. Then he was behind her, touching up her arse, the disgusting pig.

Slowly, he took off his jacket and placed it on the chair, standing in front of her for what must have seemed an eternity, torturing her by making her wait for the inevitable. Then suddenly he was all over her, grabbing at her breasts, sucking on her tits while his hand groped between her luscious thighs. She looked frightened as she struggled fruitlessly against him.

The woman in black was sitting on the edge of the desk just watching. The guy fumbled with his trousers and they dropped to the floor, his bare arse just peeking out beneath his shirt tails. I couldn't see how big his cock was but by the look on the woman's face it must have been huge. He threw off his shirt, then stood before her naked, feasting on her body.

He grabbed her by the hips and swinging her into his body, then lifted her legs and held them up around his waist so they dangled against his back. It looked like he slapped her thigh and then her legs crossed over and he began to thrust in and out of her like a dog, humping her while his face buried itself into her cleavage.

My cock was aching so I undid my zip and gave it a stroke. It responded by hardening even further so I gave it a bit of a pull while continuing to watch. I felt guilty but it was fucking great.

He began to fuck her harder. The woman on the desk flexed the whip and it sailed across his back. A red welt came up instantly. She continued to whip him, lashing his arse and thighs as well. He fucked harder, the woman bouncing all over the place and then suddenly he arched, held his position for a moment before collapsing against the woman, pressing her into the wall.

Fuck! I couldn't believe what I'd just witnessed. What the hell was going on?

The guy dressed quickly and left the room. The one hanging seemed to be laughing while the one in black picked up the whip and began to push the handle against her slit. She struggled against her restraints, not laughing now, seeming to be annoyed. The one in black kneeled before her, lifting one leg to throw over her shoulder, while she pushed the handle in and out of her pussy.

She stopped struggling and smiled, especially when she dropped the whip and her fingers seemed to be fiddling with her clit. Her head lolled back and her pelvis pushed forward, grinding against her hand. She rubbed furiously and my mouse's mouth opened, her breasts heaved and then she was shuddering, obviously orgasming.

The woman in black released her from her ropes and removed the handcuffs. Her legs wobbled for a moment and then they were all over each other, tearing off the ripped clothing and removing the leather clad mistress's attire, as money fluttered all over the floor.

Man, she had the most gorgeous body. Her massive tits were being crushed while they grappled with each other at the desk. The so-called mouse whom had been tied up, threw the other one on top of the desk, splayed her legs wide open and devoured her pussy like a hungry wolf.

She bent over, her puckered hole staring back at me. The blonde on the desk was saying something, trying to drag the other up. She climbed up her body, onto the desk as well, her knees straddling her as she bowed over to kiss her. Now I could see her fat, hairless pussy lips, still glistening with her juices, and I watched mesmerized as she lowered her pussy down, grinding it over the other's.

Their breasts were mashed together, their hands clutching and caressing. I pulled my cock, feeling my balls tighten at this spectacle before it rose to another level. The woman on top manoeuvred herself over until she was balancing in the sixty-nine position. I wondered if anyone else in my building was watching them. I was amazed at their inhibitions and their voyeuristic antics.

It was too much for me and I shot my load all over the carpet and the window. I've never been so turned on in my life. What those two women did to each other was the most fucking horny thing I've ever seen anywhere in the world, and I've seen lots. Now I work late as much as I can, hoping they'll be playing their little game again soon.

This city is certainly turning out to be the most interesting by far.

The Wages Of Bliss
by AstridL

Light fell in dapples through the leaves of the willows by
my secret pool in the glade by the baths of the mortals. It
was just after noontime and all was still as I slipped
between the silken sheets of cool water.

I floated a moment and then ducked under, my eyes wide
open beneath the surface, and watched tiny bubbles pearl
from my nostrils. I came up for air and stroked towards my
favourite clump of white lilies.

How I loved to bend them forward, dip my hand into
their waxy chalices and stroke the firm stamen until my
fingers were coated with a powdery satin. I was exploring
their slippery feel and breathing in their yeasty scent when I
heard giggles.

Two servant girls from the baths on the hill were
approaching my sun pool. I quickly kissed one of the lilies
and dipped back into the water, my head hidden behind a
curtain of willow.

"What can it mean?" one servant girl said as she sat
down at the water's edge and pulled back her *chiton* to
paddle her feet.

"The seed of Zeus will be born," said the other as she
rinsed a sheer fabric.

"Of course it will," the first said with a warm laugh.

"Don't be blasphemous," said the other. "It is said that

his seed will spell his demise," she added and proceeded to spread the sopping cloth in the sunshine.

"Only if it is a man," said the other, lying back on the mossy shore. "There was a man today ..."

"There were many," her friend said. "How many did you do?"

I, too, had heard the oracle, but it was a sacred thing, a matter for the gods, not for nymphs, and no matter for mortals. How could these girls speak in this way of great Zeus?

The girls' heads came together and they seemed to be whispering, their giggles pop popping gently like bubbles.

I strained to hear more, but to no avail, for to come closer would betray my presence. So I closed my eyes to imagine what they might have been saying.

I admit that mortals and their primal needs, so similar, in a way, to those of the gods, did fascinate me. The gods, too, I thought, might sometimes have wished to enjoy moments less marked by the epics, which by nature were their lot.

What could be more natural, I reasoned, than to still my curiosity by observing the mortals in a habitat close to my own? What could be more propitious than the baths on the hill? The bathhouse had often afforded me much pleasurable time as it was there that I would secretly watch the men congregate.

The women, like the two I had been watching, would serve the men as though they were gods. Young women with slender ankles like my own would undulate in sheer *chitons* by the edge of tiled pools. After bathing in the warm limpid waters, the men beckoned them. With the fleeces of young lambs, the women would dry the men's bodies and caress and massage their strong torsos until they glowed with a warm, bronze patina.

Their ministrations completed, the women withdrew for a time and on returning bore platters of sweetmeats, shellfish, and olives, grapes and slices of plump pomegranates. And they would feed their masters the tasty morsels and pour them black wine, a liquid more potent than the ambrosia of the gods. Then they sang and danced seductively until the men reached for them and drew them close to partake of fervent couplings.

When I opened my eyes from this reverie the two servant girls had gone; the sheer fabric they had left behind, no doubt to finish drying in the sun.

Overcome by a new and strange need, I suddenly longed to go with them, even substitute myself for one of theirs. I had learned much from my observations, but it was not enough my curiosity told me, as it now drove me forward. So I took the cloth, still damp, draped it over my breasts and knotted it at my nape.

By the time I arrived at the baths' shady portico, my covering was dry. I glanced down a moment to smooth it and saw how proudly my darkened nipples wore the attire, curious, too, in their own thrilling way.

Past the portico in a central courtyard, two men were sparring. Their bodies gleamed with sweat through caked patches of dirt and their breathing was quick. The two servant girls approached and I hid behind a sculpted pillar. With a curved metal implement they scraped the dirt-clogged oil from the men's bodies. Judging by their low moans of pleasure, the men were enjoying these attentions. Then the servants plucked fleece-like towels from a basket and led the men to the next segment of the baths. Discreetly, I followed.

Now immersed in steaming tubs, the men stretched languorously, sighed and soon closed their eyes. The warm air was drenched with the scent of olives and sweet sour excretions. So drowsy had the men now become that this must have signalled the servants to retire until further need.

Furtively, I followed the women into the next part of the

59

baths. It was a spacious closed-in arena with an elongated pool in its centre. A man languidly parted the water as he swam. Deciding that I would be less conspicuous if I did not try to hide, I slowly skirted the walls. They were adorned with mosaics and paintings depicting the play of nymphs and satyrs. The ceiling was high and vaulted and the soft marbled hues of salmon and green recalled the subsurface life of my pool in the glade. The air was still warm, but it was imbued with a delicious new fragrance of jasmine and musk. The lap lapping of the swimmer, the intoxicating closeness of the humid air made me dizzy with a hitherto unknown form of arousal.

"You are new here," said a man I had never before seen and grabbed at my wrist. I wriggled free, then, calming, said, yes, it was so.

"Come dry me then," he said.

He was tall and strong, his head a mass of golden curls. His beard likewise. His lips were full and generous and his eyes were the colour of midnight.

I quivered on seeing droplets of water trickle down his firm chest past his hipbone to disappear into more golden curls of a coarser nature. A crown of fresh ivy dipped from his fingers, but I was too taken to wonder at that.

He motioned me away from the pool to a high bench of marble that gave out on a vista of olive groves. "I am waiting," he said as he lay down and closed his eyes.

I could but comply. So I took the fluffiest of fleeces and proceeded to blot his body – his chest, his torso and down to his thighs where an appendage I hitherto had not seen from this distance stiffened and proudly grew. I knew it to be named phallus, but the veins, barely visible, seemed to net his whole being. I drew back. The man laughed and rolled onto his stomach, exposing the tightest of buttock mounds.

"Proceed," he said with a warm roll to his voice.

No longer having his gaze to contend with, I looked about me. Apart from one or two benches on the other side of the pool where women rhythmically attended to their masters, the baths were empty save for the lone swimmer. The only sounds were the dampened echoes of soft moans and sighs, and the fresh gentle slapping of water against the green mosaic of the pool.

Entranced, I poured virginal oil scented with olives into my palms and commenced my first massage. I drew up my robe and climbed onto the bench, my knees astride him, and let my weight guide my long strokes. His muscles relaxed under my hands. The effect seemed to please him, and this was borne out by his words, "How good that does feel", to which I could but return my own murmur of pleasure, and proceed.

After a time, during which I addressed his back and buttocks, I alighted, came around to his head and massaged his upper back and shoulders. Perspiration trickled between my breasts, blotting the sheerness of my covering. The man's spine made me think of the central strong vein in a leaf of ivy and I could not help tracing a finger along its course.

Suddenly, through the fabric of my apparel, he lightly stroked my stomach. Thrills feathered through me. Then he reached for my buttocks and held them, not fiercely but with a firm touch. I heard the silence of strings, that silence before a tone is sounded, and pretending that I had not noticed, I proceeded to run my hands along his arms, ending with his hands and the tips of his fingers, and hoping he would not sense my own fingertips tingling.

During the course of these ministrations in which all sound dissipated I encountered the strange sensation that he was opening his mind to me, that I might even be able to enter his thoughts, perhaps read them, a prospect, which could but thrill my curiosity. The waters of my birth having

61

taught me the need of giving myself to the flow, I applied more oil to work on his legs as I had seen the servant girls do.

I was standing at about the mid of the bench when I felt a light touching of my own legs through the folds of my covering. I felt his touch on my inner thighs. Again, his mind seemed to open and I became privy to secret thoughts of what I perceived to be a dilemma, arising perhaps from a conflict between the needs of his mind and that of his phallus, now speaking out the most primal of needs, one I, too, had to admit. Yet, he seemed governed by a singular code of civility, perhaps even good manners, since he did not demand with the force I had seen used by other men in the baths. Given his sighs and the words in his mind, this dilemma must have steered those moments of waxing and waning of the precious appendage. I concentrated on attuning my mind to his thoughts: Was she ruled by a master? Where did she live? She was new here. Not experienced. Somehow ruled by an innocent passion. Delightful.

Puzzled, yet touched by this internal conflict, I untied the knot in my nape and let my clothing slide to the floor. Then I climbed back upon the bench to attend to his legs. After some time I then turned and could not resist tantalizing him by running my nipples, like fingers, up and down his back.

Eventually I climbed down and worked more on his legs. Now running my hands more lightly than before, I brought my fingers along the insides of his thighs and, making the slightest, briefest contact, ran a fingernail over the scrotum. Every fibre of his being seemed concentrated on that one area, and this slightest of attentions had a great effect, apparent from an accelerating stiffening. That stiffening now dispelled the former waxing and waning which, no doubt, had been due to the physical experience vying with a succession of random thoughts. But those thoughts had related to my own being, and I could only feel tenderness for this mortal and so needed to speak. Yet all I could say was: "Will you now want turn over?" He did so, with alacrity and I knew I must change my approach.

I lightened my strokes and centred them around the tops of his thighs and lower abdomen, carefully skirting that other brain already awaiting a life of its own. My charms were now fully within reach and the man had free range of my breasts, should he so desire. And desire he did and did proceed with distinct pleasure to stroke and to tease them, to which ministrations my nipples answered with their own stiffening.

In due course my hands, fresh-slicked with oil, brushed more and more frequently, always slowly, sensuously, against scrotum and phallus which I must now call cock, so proud did it stand, enough to put any dawn rooster to shame. Thus far silence had reigned, but then he said: "You are very, very good". This pleased me, which he must have seen in the way I gently pursued my actions. And so his own hands now became alive, one taking increasing, almost feverish interest in my labia, gathering moisture thereupon, penetrating, exploring my clitoris (which could not help swelling), and then once again a mind intrusion: "How often is she prone to such arousal? What is the effect upon her? Does she even notice? Perhaps it is just how her body attends to business."

To block out his thoughts, my hands became more purposeful, still moving slowly but with deliberation. How I longed to take the luscious tip into my mouth, but I did not, could not dare.

Presently, his body took on a curious syncopated rhythm of its own, a kind of instinctive reflexive movement overwhelmed, one clearly destined for the procreative act. I watched enthralled as this display inexorably led to a coming of the juices of his own type of ambrosia, a coming which his mind showed me was in itself equal to that of more preferred circumstances. My pulse throbbed as my own dreams of such circumstance battled the folly of being locked in as a servant.

With a release of the hand, I slowly, gently, brought things to an end. "I shall fetch a hot towel," I said leaving him on his back, smiling and visibly satisfied.

My thoughts were in turmoil and in need of examination as I plucked the fabric from the marble floor, slipped it on and knotted it once more. How could I dream of more from this mortal? Would my life change back at my pool now that I knew this new hunger?

When I returned he was almost in slumber so I ministered tenderly, intending soon to depart, but knowing that I needed to leave him clean and with comfort, a comfort that I had no right to know.

Then he spoke: "Bring me food and the sweetest of wines now."

Relieved in a way from a certain thrill, and with the feeling I might still prolong my sojourn, I left to do his bidding. I returned with a pitcher of black wine and a platter of fresh abalone, the most delicate of shellfish that like all of their kind had a hidden pearl. I also brought olives, and the shiniest, reddest grapes I could find.

"Peel me one," he said.

So I sat by his side and gingerly peeled the membrane from the plump fruit, exposing its glistening succulence.

"Feed me," he said, and I complied. His lips closed over my fingers as he drew the naked grape into his mouth – it was almost as if to feed upon me. We continued thus until the silver platter was spent. Then he drank from the wine. When he was sated he reached for my hand. I trembled, but he insisted.

And so he led me to a canopy in a secluded corner of the baths. Parting a long curtain, he revealed a broad, low couch covered in silks of the greens and the blues of my pool in the glade.

He drew me close and his fingers stroked the knot at my nape. I remained still, my heart thrilling as his hands explored the secrets of my untouched body through the folds of the fabric still covering it. He cupped my breasts, plucked at my nipples, squeezing with the gentlest of forces that transported me with shivers of delight. Although he had just eaten, his lips seemed possessed of a hunger I wished was now ready to feed upon me. His curious fingers continued their descent to find my nectar waiting to drip. He moaned in approval and I closed my eyes. And then that which was the proud cocking appendage proceeded to thrust and to pump, swallowed in full by my ravenous vulva.

As he peeled back my clothing I once again heard his mind: I saw how he felt the silk of my skin, inhaled me, visually bathed in my curves and the contrast of my pale breasts, the madder areoles. And tasting his lips, his tongue, all for me, too, became a wild dream coming true.

Enveloped by sweet sounds of a breeze swishing through willows and the lap-lapping of the nearby pool, the warm scent of sweet ginger joining musk and jasmine, I found myself totally within the moment, without past or future, my being centred in all my senses.

We trailed kisses over each other, and at last I took him into my mouth, where I held him, sucked, licked and drank him. And, like a hummingbird feasting on honeysuckle, he then dipped his tongue into me.

And so we touched and tasted our way to the moment at which I had to beg him to enter which he, wholly possessed, did, although at first with restraint. He just nudged between my labia, rubbing, tormenting me, and as I ached and urged to have him within me, he plunged deep. Then he tantalized, teased, his strokes building exquisite tension and to pre-empt surely an untimely explosion. Yet all was imbued with a charming but woeful innocence.

My fingernails scored his back, my hips thrust; I wailed and, unable to hold back any longer, his pace frenzied. I felt him swell within me, and then the hot bursts of his seed irrupted, then slowed, and he became still, still tumescent, and we both, almost still, too, panted just slightly, sweat dewing our faces, conjoining our skin as we lay together. And in that moment, as his senses retreated, faster even than his quiet dissipation, past and future suddenly blended.

"Delightful servant," he moaned.

And I, no longer able to maintain my subterfuge, whispered: "Dear mortal, dear mortal."

And it was this chance remark that, as I read it, forced his vision of me, his goddess, to be in reality no such thing at all. I truly felt thus as I saw worry and fear, yes, disillusionment even, now crowding pell-mell into the mental vacuum of our spent lust. Suddenly I yearned to go back in time to the point at which he had given in to that most urgent signal of his procreative organ.

He pulled back, saying nothing, and gazed into my eyes.

Quietly, I said: "I am, dear mortal, not the servant you think."

Yet he did but smile and then kiss me. "And I, dear being, am but the god Zeus."

I pulled back.

"I also enjoy the sports of the mortals," he said as he stroked my cheek. "You now, dear being, you carry my seed. And that is your due, for I have opened to you the secrets of my mind."

My senses atumble, it was then that I recognised the thrust of the oracle and how I had become its treacherous instrument.

"Dear Zeus. It must not be. Thy seed grows within me to overcome thee."

Zeus gazed at me and with a broad palm stroked my hair. "I am smitten by you and you have been honest with me. And yet …" He kept stroking but I could only tremble. Then he smiled. "I may have a solution," he said. "But first I must once more drink of your ambrosia."

I did not fully understand what he meant, but when his hands resumed their gentle ministrations, when he parted my legs and nuzzled my core, his lips suckling, sucking, the delight of his tongue and his fingers probing my innermost reaches, I was once more fully transported into the flow of another life.

When I came to my senses, I was within him, swallowed into the belly of Zeus. No longer would I be able to delight in our couplings, but for this I had been ready to pay the price.

The oracle, I knew, could now not come true, for his seed, no longer only within me, was now within him. He would have, I foresaw, his own share of suffering.

His head, captive of the worry he tried to control, would be beset by most terrible pain. The Titan, Prometheus, would strike his cranium with one mighty blow and a goddess in the likeness of Zeus would emerge, fully clothed, clad in armour, but of a beauty quiet and firm. She would be just and she would be fair, as her father was unto me. She would be well versed in the weaving from fleeces and would prepare the most delicious of meals. All this and more would be Athena, the fruit of our coupling in the baths of the mortals.

And I, the nymph, Metis, no mortal, no goddess, would outlive Hera, the wife of his life. I would outlive all those he pursued in search of the bliss for which I was the keeper. I would remain deep within him, forever close to the heart and never far from the mind of my lover, the mighty god, Zeus.

Art Of Seduction
by Gina Martinelli

Paris, September 1793

Angelique's heart pounded as the carriage rumbled along the cobble stones. She could not believe how her life had changed so drastically. France was in turmoil. The revolution had come.

"At least we escaped with our lives," she murmured, thinking of her loyal servants who had stayed behind. If it hadn't been for them, hiding her in a secret passage, she would have been murdered by the villagers who had stormed the Chateau.

"They are killing aristocrats everywhere," said the woman, sitting beside her.

"I know. But perhaps in Paris we will be safer." Angelique's fingers trembled as she pushed aside the square piece of curtain on the carriage window. Through the small space she could see Notre Dame looming up, the gargoyles glaring at her as they passed.

A mob of men congregated on the corner, their faces bitter and twisted as they turned to look at the carriage. Angelique let the curtain fall, but not before she had seen a man turn, his features outlined by the burning torch held in his right hand. He had jet black hair, touching his shoulders, and high cheekbones. Even in the shadowy light, she could see his skin was pale as he addressed the mob. He waved his arms in fury at the carriage. Several police officers stood beside him, their weapons held across their chests.

The carriage picked up speed. Angry shouts echoed around her. Pistol shots pierced the air.

"Oh my God...they are after us again," said her companion.

Angelique put a reassuring hand on the woman's arm. "Do not fear so. Our driver is the best. He will not let them catch us." She paused slightly, saying softly, "And even if they did, I would use these."

She held up a pair of silver pistols that she had placed under the seat. They were weapons that belonged to her father, gifted to him by the King to show his appreciation for the finest wine her father had supplied the Royal House from his Loire Valley vineyard.

"It is best I make my own way, Mademoiselle," the woman said. Earlier on, Angelique had offered her refuge at their house in Paris, but she had declined. The carriage slowed, and then stopped. The last thing Angelique saw was the woman's black cloak swirling about her as she blended into a dark alleyway.

Angelique thought about her father. She had rarely seen him over the past year as he had been travelling around Europe. She knew perfectly well he had plans to marry her off to a man who was twice her age and very rich. But she wouldn't let him, she thought adamantly. She wanted to marry for love as she had often read about in the books she had bought every time she had visited Paris.

The carriage pulled up with a jolt. Wearily, Angelique made her way up the steps to her father's residence.

"This way, Mademoiselle..." the maid said with a quick curtsy, showing her to her bedchamber. Angelique sank onto the four-poster bed and closed her eyes, grateful to have made it to safety.

The maid hovered. "Shall I help you undress, Mademoiselle?"

Angelique gave a smile. "Non. Merci."

"You would like a cup of cocoa?"

"Oui, s'il vous plaît"

She was just drifting off to sleep a few minutes later when the maid returned. She seemed agitated. "'Are you awake, Mademoiselle? There is a man downstairs who demands to see you."

"Me?" Angelique's brow creased in puzzlement. "But what could he possibly want?"

The maid shook her head. "I do not know."

When Angelique entered the salon, she froze. She couldn't believe her eyes. It was he. The man she had seen on the street corner earlier.

He gave a bow. "My name is Adrien Laroche. I am a Senior officer on the Committee of General Security." He paused briefly. "I have some questions I would like to ask you. Please…" he pointed to a chair, "won't you be seated."

Angelique knew that he would be under the authority of Robespierre, the most feared man in all of France.

The man cleared his throat. "Robespierre has given orders…"

"Robespierre," she cut in with disgust. "That murderer. He executed the King, and now he wants rid of the Queen."

His jaw tightened. "Mademoiselle, I advise you to be careful in what you say."

Refusing to be intimidated, she held his gaze. "But it is true. I am not afraid to voice my opinion."

"Brave words, but foolish," he murmured. Laroche moved forward, so that he towered over her where she sat. Angelique could feel the ruthless strength emanating from him as he circled her slowly. She bit her lip, holding down the thudding apprehension in her chest.

"Why are you here, in Paris?" he demanded. "Do you

71

not realise how dangerous it is to travel the roads at night?"

"We had no choice." She told him what had happened. "My father had sent word a few days ago he would be here. But as you see, he is not."

Suddenly he reached out and grabbed her wrist. "You lie. Where is he?"

Her breath came in a gasp. "I do not know." She tried to loosen his grip but he would not let her go.

He said softly, a hint of steel in his voice. "Do you know what the Conciergerie is, Mademoiselle?

Her throat went dry. "Yes," she whispered. "I know of it." It was where traitors are taken to be tortured.

"Then you had better be telling me the truth."

"I am. My father has not done anything wrong. I am sure of it. He is a law-abiding citizen."

"That is not what I have heard. Your father is working against the revolution."

"No, you are wrong. He would never do such a thing. He looks after those who work for him. I cannot believe he would be involved in anything like you are insinuating."

"Your devotion is very touching," he said dryly.

Angelique gave him a defiant look, but her pulse was racing.

Laroche fingered the ruby necklace around her neck, making her quiver. The stones glowed deep red in the flickering candlelight. He touched her neck, his cool fingers sliding across her pale white shoulders. The touch of his fingers reminded her of the guillotine. So many had died already. She was innocent, so she had nothing to fear, she reminded herself.

"A pretty necklace, Mademoiselle, n'est-ce pas?" he said. "And for one as beautiful as you."

"'It was a present from my mother before she died," explained Angelique.

He moved behind her and unfastened the necklace. The

touch of those long fingers upon her skin made her heart beat faster. He took the rubies from her neck and moved away from her chair, holding the stones steadily in the palm of his hand.

"These stones are worth a great deal. The money they could bring would feed many families," he remarked, irony in his tone. "Have you no shame?"

She took a deep breath. "I would not wish people to starve..."

As Laroche leaned closer she could see the tiny lines of exhaustion around his eyes. His shoulders set with weariness. "We will see if your heart is true, or whether the blood that runs in your veins is as hard as these stones." He turned to the guard in the corner and said harshly, "Arrest her."

Two days she had been locked up in this room. Angelique battered on the door with her fists. Suddenly, the lock rattled and the door opened. It was Adrien Laroche, the officer who had arrested her.

"Leave us," he said to the guard. The door slammed shut behind him. "So..." he began, "has this spell of confinement brought you to your senses?"

Angelique lifted her chin. "I have done nothing. You have no right to keep me here."

He gave a small laugh. "Ah...we shall see." His finger stroked her cheek. "You are trembling, Mademoiselle."

"I...I...am feeling cold. There were not enough blankets."

He frowned. "I had given orders you were to be made comfortable."

Her pulse rioted at his concern. His nearness was disconcerting and she tried to look away but it was impossible. She could feel his gaze raking her. If only she had her shawl with her, to cover herself. She felt so exposed

73

in her black silk dress, the bodice laced provocatively low.

He reached behind her, pulling the pins from her hair so it fell loose around her shoulders. She was at his mercy and he knew it.

He gave a laugh. "Yes, you are my prisoner, Mademoiselle. And your father is also in my custody."

"My father?" she gasped, forgetting about her own discomforts. "You have found him?"

His eyes narrowed. "He has admitted his guilt."

"You forced him," she accused.

"No..." he said sharply. "He confessed readily. Of course, he had encouragement. He knew you had been imprisoned."

Angelique fell silent. After a few moments, she asked carefully, "What do you want with me now?"

"Simple. I have a proposal to make." His eyes flickered. "I wish you to spend a night with me. In return, I will ensure your father's sentence of the guillotine will be changed to ten years in gaol."

She looked at him steadily. "And if I refuse?"

"Your father will die. And you will be sold into a brothel."

Angelique stared. "You cannot mean it."

"Mademoiselle, I will give you time to think about my proposal. But not too long. I am an impatient man."

He had just turned towards the door, when she said, "Wait..." She took a step forward, her mind made up. "I will do as you say."

What could she expect from him, she wondered? Every possibility ran through her mind.

"Come," said Laroche, taking her arm firmly. He led her to the carriage. When they arrived at his apartment, she was fascinated to see it littered with papers and books. He opened a bottle of white wine and poured her a glass. "Let us toast to our bargain."

She took the glass from him, and studied the label on the bottle. "Oh…this is wine from our vineyard."

"Very appropriate, do you not think? It is my favourite wine. It has a tang. Fruity and smooth." He leaned closer. "It thrills the palate like the kiss of a lover." His words were said so sensuously that Angelique could not help flushing. Would he even guess she had never even been kissed before? But she was not about to tell him this. She sipped the wine slowly, grateful for the time that it bought her before the inevitable. All those books of love she had read would be of no help to her now.

On the wooden table lay a pair of iron handcuffs. Her eyes widened. Would he intend using them on her should she resist? The thought of them made her breath come in quicker.

As if he knew what she was thinking, Laroche lifted them up and shook them so they jangled. "For you? No. You are too fine boned for these. I would not wish to chafe that delicate skin of yours."

"Oh…" was all she could say in confusion. His gentle manner seemed at odds with his earlier attitude. It was obvious he was a complex man. Perhaps, in time she could learn more about him.

"You know Robespierre well?" she asked tentatively.

"Well enough…" He gave a frown.

"He is a butcher," she stated with vehemence.

"He once was a visionary," he replied quickly. "Is it so wrong to want justice for our people?" His eyes burned with an intensity that took her breath away. "I have given my life to this cause. To free France from the burden of the aristocracy. Equality for all."

"The world thinks otherwise."

He shot a blistering look at her. "Who cares what the world thinks?" He put his hand on his chest, over his heart. "I am a Frenchman. It is what we feel here. That is what counts."

If only a man would be as passionate about her as he was about his cause.

"Your vision has led to a bloodbath," she reminded him.

"I did not want this to happen…but," he shrugged resigned, "those who hold the power will not change willingly. So they will be forced to. It is the only way."

"Like you are forcing me," she said suddenly.

She was rewarded with an angry glint in his eyes. He caught her wrist. "Damn you, Angelique. Your tongue has an acid touch about it. It is time to teach you a lesson."

She didn't go willingly. He lifted her and deposited her roughly on the bed. She immediately scrambled off but he caught her around her waist and held her in his arms.

"Need I remind you about your father?" he whispered in her ear.

She froze, her heart hammering wildly.

She let him unlace her bodice. She could not help but notice his fingers, long and tapering. Angelique felt her nipples tighten, and through the silky material she knew Adrien could see it as well. The corners of his mouth lifted.

Once she was in her shift, his hands slipped under her full breasts cupping them, the fingertips smoothing over her taut nipples in a teasing caress.

"Ah, you like this, do you not?" he said.

"I…I…" she stammered. A whirlwind of emotions shot through her.

As she looked at him, she realised how attracted she was to the deepness of his smile and the darkness of his eyes. To her shock, she found her own hands ached to undo his shirt, to feel the hardness of his muscled chest against the softness of her own skin. Then, as if he was aware of her feelings, he gave a small, knowing laugh.

"We will take our time," he added softly.

Summoning up her courage, she undid his buttons,

76

slowly, one by one. But with an impatient groan he ripped his shirt apart, the remainder of the buttons scattering in all directions. He grabbed her hand and pressed it against his midriff.

"Touch me here," he demanded, and she did, smoothing her hand across the planes of his stomach, until he groaned with sheer pleasure. It gave her a sense of power that she could have this effect on him.

With one sweep of his other hand, he cupped her arse. Even with the folds of her skirts in the way, she could feel the hard swell of his cock against her, throbbing and pulsing. A deep, aching need opened inside her as her heart started racing, and her nerve endings began sizzling. She could feel her own wetness below, and the wanting of him. Her own body had finally betrayed her, she realised.

With her skirts pooled on the floor, she waited, only imagining what would come next. He stepped out of his breeches and she could not help but stare at his nakedness. The broadness of his chest emphasised his waist tapering to slim hips. She dropped her gaze, uncertain as to what to do, but not before she had seen his cock, erect, and moist at the tip. Her breath began to quicken. She could not think properly. It is the wine, she thought. Or was it sorcery? Perhaps he had drugged her. Yet in all honesty, she knew he would not be the type of man to use drugs or the black arts. It would be a matter of pride where a woman was concerned.

A suffused warmth crept down her body as his forefinger traced a path from her neck, downwards across her breasts to that secret part of her between her thighs. She gave a gasp at the sudden unfamiliarity of his touch, but after a few moments her tension eased as his movement gentled, caressing the silky folds. She began to throb. A small strangled sound came from her throat.

"It is not so bad, n'est-ce pas?" he teased. "I think you

are ready for me."

She wasn't going to be a virgin much longer, she realised. Wasn't this what she had wanted all along?

She tried to deny the pulsing knot in her stomach.

"Lie on your front," he said softly. Cautiously, she turned. He grabbed a pillow and placed it under her hips so they tilted upwards. His hands smoothed over the curves of her arse. A part of her felt excitement, another fear. It was a heady mixture. She recalled a novel she had read called the 'Art of Seduction' and although she lacked experience she had read of the ways between lovers and marvelled at it.

Something hard penetrated her gently at first, then with his arm around her hips, he lifted her, moving his cock deeper inside. She could not help but cry out at the unfamiliarity of it.

"Am I too rough?" he asked her, pausing.

Had she been mistaken in hearing a note of concern in his voice?

She shook her head. "No…no…it was just that you caught me by surprise." That was true, she thought. He had. "Oh…" she murmured, giving in to the pleasurable feeling as he continued slowly sliding in and out in a rhythmic motion. His shaft seemed to fill her completely. The tension in her stomach disappeared replaced with wanton abandon. She found her hips instinctively responding by arching with each of his thrusts. He cupped her breasts, whispering in her ear, sucking and teasing with his tongue along the softness of her neck.

"Now…turn around," he demanded, "lie on your back," and slowly, wickedly teasing him, she did. Moving upwards, he lay his shaft between her breasts before trailing down to between her thighs where he nestled. He nudged her legs wider with his knee. With his weight on his elbows, he penetrated her, his cock stiff and big still. The force of him made her gasp. With one hand he grabbed her wrists and held them above her head. A cry screamed in her throat at the delicious sensation accompanying each thrust. He moved harder, deeper, faster. She could feel his balls smacking into her. Then he gave one long thrust that set his jaw tight.

His weight was heavy upon her, but she was more conscious of a warm feeling pooling within her. He shifted, withdrawing his cock, the wetness coating her thighs. Gasping for air, he lay on his side and looked at her.

He raised his brow.

She couldn't help but smile.

Unable to prevent herself touching him, her hand crept lower, straight to his cock, which now lay still. Within seconds of her touch, he began to harden again.

"You want more?" he asked, surprised.

Her gaze found his. "Yes. But let me..." She sat up, kneeling beside him as he lay flat on his back.

She would show him she was no simpering young girl, but a woman who could keep her side of the bargain. It would be a night he wouldn't forget. Even though he had forced her consent in the beginning, she did not see why she could not take the initiative now.

Beads of moisture topped the end of his cock as she bent over to curl her lips around him. Her tongue caressed, smoothing over the delicate tip.

"You're tormenting me," he said tightly, gripping her shoulder.

"No more than what you had intended for me," she said in a husky tone.

He gave a laugh that sent a thrill down her spine. She straddled him, slipping him in quickly. She moved up and down, hard and fast. His hands slaked against her hips gripping her tight. Just as he was about to climax, he took her by surprise, flipping her onto her back.

"Now I have you," he whispered. His mouth closed over

her nipple sucking hard. They moved in unison, each thrust sending her pulse skyward. Her nails scraped down his back. She had no idea that love-making could be like this. She could not talk. Nor could she breathe. All she could think about was him inside her and the sensations that tore at her one by one.

Sweat slicked her body. He traced his tongue across her breasts and upwards to her mouth where his tongue played and tantalized. Another thrust with his hips and she could tell he was near the edge. She was so wet, dripping. The sheet dampened beneath her.

He shouted her name as he came.

Panting hard, she lay back against the covers, watching his chest rise and fall, both of them gasping for air.

A masterful lover, she thought. And I, his novice.

Eventually, when his breathing steadied and so did hers, he turned onto his side, and looked at her steadily.

"You are different," he said.

Her heart danced. "Perhaps, because you want me to be."

He shook his head. "No, it is something else…something indefinable." He gave her a thoughtful look. "I have another proposal," he began.

Excitement shot through her. "Go on."

"I need a wife."

She jolted. "A wife?"

He nodded. "If you marry me, I will see to it your father will be exiled instead of spending ten years in gaol."

She had not expected marriage. Yet, she guessed his proposal was more than that. Working for Robespierre he would have seen such horrors, such depravity. How could she blame him for wanting to find solace in a woman's arms. So…was she to be the balm that laid his soul to rest? But why her, she wondered? Still, she was shocked to find it was a role she could easily contemplate. And her father would be free.

But what of love, she reasoned.

"There is more," he added, as if he sensed her doubts. "We will become part of the new France. Liberated. As my wife, you will be at my side always."

A thrill shot through her. Nights of passion. Status. He would fall in love with her eventually. She was sure of it. Dare she think that perhaps he already had.

She nodded, her gaze holding his. "I can understand your ideals." He had been noble once. But no-one who had fought so long in the cause of freedom could remain unscathed. The shadows in his eyes told her that the ghosts would be with him until eternity.

"I want all of you," he added, reaching for her, urgency in his love-making.

Almost a declaration of love, she thought hopefully. He grabbed fistfuls of her hair as he lifted himself, and plundered her mouth, his stubbled cheek hard against hers. He whispered words which made her blush. Angelique, too shocked at her own response, reacted instinctively. She opened for him, releasing a soft moan that drove him on.

"So what's it to be?" he whispered in her ear.

"Yes, yes." Her body arched to meet him, entwining strongly with his.

Later, as they settled amongst the disarray of bed covers, both shaken with their passion, she had to ask him. "You have known other women?"

"Some…" But that was all he would say on the matter. "But now there is only you."

He turned her face towards him, using the moon's light to see as the candle on the table had long since melted into a pool of wax. "Ma chérie." *My darling.*

Was this what it was like to be loved? Her hand touched his cheek as he lay back against the lacy pillow. He caught her hand, his lips skimming her palm in the tenderest of kisses, and then his fingers linked tightly with hers.

"Life will not be the same," he said softly.

"I am not afraid," she answered, her gaze shifting, settling on the iron handcuffs lying on the table.

He smiled. "Somehow, I did not think you would be."

La Zingarella
by Fransiska Sherwood

La Zingarella was going to be something special. Small and chic. Classy, but not too pricey. A place known for the excellence of its cuisine. And the allure of its flamboyant hostess.

Rosella turned the sign on the door to read 'open'. Her heart fluttered. It was their first night. Would the restaurant do well? The enterprise was a gamble. It wasn't the only Italian osteria in town by any means, and competition was already fierce.

Rosella peeped into the tiny alley. Apart from a swirl of russet leaves blowing round the cobbles, it was empty. How many guests might she hope for tonight? Without a good write-up in the restaurant guides you couldn't expect to lure crowds – even with a free glass of prosecco.

But Rosella didn't want to lure crowds, anyway. More the discerning few. She wasn't catering for the pizza and tortellini crew. That segment was already well covered.

She crossed herself, and kissed the rosary hanging round her neck for luck. Those smooth, round, well-fingered beads the women in her family had always put their faith in when it counted. But nothing was going to go wrong that night. Bruno had been in the kitchen, chopping and peeling, mixing and stirring, since four. He really was an angel. A find in a million. A genius. Whatever mouth-watering temptation Rosella might conjure up in her head, Bruno could recreate it on the plate. Elaborate seafood platters; artichokes stuffed with polenta and pine kernels; bruschetta spread with dried tomato pesto; panna cotta drizzled in a bitter, mocca sauce. Dishes to transport you to heaven. Desserts that were pure sin.

And the greatest sin of all was his tiramisù. No one made anything comparable. Mesmerized, Rosella had watched him prepare a whole pan-full that very afternoon. With greedy eyes she'd traced the pattern left by his whisk as he stirred the crème. Always in the same direction, with the endless patience of an indulgent lover, so as not to destroy its exquisite, fluffy texture. Then he'd spread it with swift, even strokes over the sponge fingers, lavished in coffee liqueur and lined up like rows of soldiers. Layer upon irresistible layer. Until finally he topped the lot with a thick coating of cocoa powder that fell from his sieve like chocolate snowflakes.

Watching him was sheer culinary seduction. Rosella had had to banish herself from the kitchen. There were too many temptations. She'd treat herself later. Indulge in anything she fancied.

Still hoping to see someone making their way towards her, Rosella hovered on the threshold for another moment. Under the lamplight the leaves twirled a forlorn pirouette, but there wasn't a soul about.

She sighed. What had she been expecting? People to come running the minute they opened?

The shimmering cerise flounces of her taffeta skirt rustled as she turned back inside, whispering consolation. Rosella went behind the bar. It wasn't good to stand waiting for people. More off-putting than inviting. She'd just have to be patient. A virtue she didn't possess.

She turned to the rows of glasses lined up on the shelves behind her and caught her image in the tiny mirrored tiles that twinkled and sparkled on the rear wall in a distorted kaleidoscope of colours.

Was her hair all right? Did the black bodice sit just as it should? Revealing enough, but not too much. Had she smudged her lipstick?

Rosella hurried to the mirror. No, everything was perfect. Just as it had been the last time she checked. Two minutes ago. And every bit as enticing as the food she offered: lips of the same cerise as her skirt, as inviting as ripe cherries and begging to be kissed; a cascade of chestnut ringlets, piled up high into a twisted knot; and dark, smouldering eyes that harboured secrets full of passion. The real-life embodiment of La Zingarella's logo. A gypsy temptress.

Maybe Bruno could do with some help?

Rosella slipped through the swing doors to the kitchen. What else was she to do? Waiting was driving her crazy.

Bruno winked as she came in. That all-knowing crease of his eye, as if they'd been in partnership for years and he could read her every thought and mood.

Were her nerves so apparent?

Okay, she was keyed up with anticipation. Like waiting for a blind date who hadn't yet showed.

'Don't let me disturb you.'

Bruno flashed her a grin.

She watched him slice a leek into delicate fronds. For such a great brute he had the lightest of touches.

Rosella smiled to herself. If she'd not found him in the kitchen wearing a white apron, she'd have suspected him of working some mafioso protection racket. The jagged scar that puckered his cheek sent a frisson through her every time she looked at him.

Rosella returned to the restaurant and started polishing glasses that already sparkled like crystal. It wouldn't do for her first guests to arrive and there be no one to welcome them.

To her relief she wasn't kept hopping from one foot to the other for much longer. A grey-haired gentleman pushed open the door and entered the restaurant. A man so grave he couldn't yet have tasted any of life's pleasures, she thought.

With a critical eye he inspected the place. Whether it met with his approval, Rosella couldn't tell.

The restaurant was one of a row of cellar premises, half at street level, with a set of steps leading down to it from the pavement. The place had been cold and damp when she first bought it and its smell had reminded her of truffles. An earthiness, laced with Beaujolais, she'd hoped to conserve. Sadly, it had been ephemeral. Now, with its candles and terracotta-stained walls, it had a cosy intimacy that just lent itself to a romantic tête-à-tête.

Rosella led the man to his table and caught the peppermint coolness of his breath.

Mint – that was a flavour not on the menu. She'd have to get Bruno to concoct something with it when the season came. Maybe a dessert of strawberries with peppermint parfait, or a salad of melon balls and mint leaves. Something for early summer. Something innocent and unadulterated which caught that freshness, and made your mouth water by its very scent. ...Something that took you back to your first kiss.

She let her mind wander as she went for the menu. Imagining for a moment she was a young shepherd girl and the scent came from crushed mint leaves, trodden underfoot as she made her way down the hillside, back to her village, after a secret rendezvous.

It was just a little bit of harmless day-dreaming, a frivolous game, and she let it go no further. Yet a thrill of excitement still rippled through her at the thought.

The man took his time choosing, although the menu was just one piece of card. A short, select list that changed with the availability of the ingredients – always seasonal and harvest-fresh. It touched Rosella to think that young farm lads went out at dawn to pick it for her. When the morning was still crisp and their beds still warm.

Finally, he decided to eat à la carte. The first of Rosella's themed menus.

*** Homage to Autumn ***
Pumpkin soup, with a hint of ginger and a
swirl of pumpkin seed oil
Guinea fowl breast on a bed of caramelised vegetables
Venison in a honey and coriander sauce,
glazed carrots and walnut gnocchi
A choice of desserts

Spectacles perched on the end of his nose, the man began to study the wine list with the same academic concentration as before.

'I'd recommend a Riesling to start with, the Chardonnay with the guinea fowl, and the Cabernet Sauvignon with the venison,' Rosella advised. She hoped he'd forgive her presumption, but she knew the best wines to accompany the meal.

The Riesling had a crisp, green-apple freshness like a clear, cold meadow stream. As she poured a glass, Rosella pictured herself in a white petticoat and camisole top dipping her toes in the icy water. Then running barefoot through the grass, pursued by a brown-eyed boy with a mop of unruly dark curls, who tumbled her among the buttercups.

Rosella cut the reverie off there as her head sank amid the petals. Before his lips came down on hers and his hands started to caress her body. ...Before she let out a sigh, or something worse, and embarrassed both herself and her guest.

This day-dreaming had got to stop.

Her mind firmly clamped on what she was doing, she brought over the wine. Then went to the kitchen for the soup. But as she carried in the steaming bowl, a whiff of ginger spiralled its way to her nostrils and, for a moment, transported her to the sultry bed of a dark, exotic lover. With skin that smelt of spices and felt like velvet. Skin that she wanted to run her tongue over...

No. Stop it. She'd promised herself she'd not think such things. It was time to get on with the job. And that was an order.

Immediately the soup turned into the swirling skirt of a flamenco dancer. Haughty and aloof. Yet full of passion. An adept player of power games.

Despite herself, as her own skirt twirled round her, Rosella couldn't help imagining she was that flamenco dancer, goading her would-be suitors to a frenzy with the light agility of her body, then turning them away with disdain.

All except, maybe, for one... A gigolo with sleek, black hair oiled to his scalp and a body that matched hers in its muscle tone and grace. An athlete well-versed in the harmonies of motion, who could lead her at will.

And she would follow his every movement, replying with her own steps. Moulding her sequences to his. The dance rapidly progressing from a tentative flirt to a torrid crescendo of desire.

A dance that didn't stop on the dance-floor.

Rosella felt her nostrils twitch as she placed the bowl in front of her guest. She checked herself just in time and reprimanded her wayward mind. Hadn't she just said she wasn't going to indulge in any more fantasies of that kind?

'Pumpkin soup with pumpkin seed oil from the Steiermark in Austria, sir.'

He gave an appreciative nod, but said nothing. A man as

antiseptic as his mouthwash – and he was beginning to annoy her. He might pretend to be a connoisseur of fine food and wine, but did he have the sensibility to appreciate an oil of such individual quality? If she were to smear his cock in it, would he appreciate it better then? He probably couldn't even imagine such a thing.

Rosella banished the errant thought immediately and turned away.

No, he probably couldn't imagine such a thing. But Rosella could. And wouldn't it make an excellent lubricant.

It was an idea she just couldn't shake out of her head.

She made her way back to the kitchen, her mind free-wheeling. Suddenly, a flaxen-haired Styrian youth popped up in front of her, like a genie out of a bottle. His chest was broad and he had a hazelnut tan from haymaking on the hillside slopes. He flashed her a fluorescent grin and his blue eyes twinkled mischief. She couldn't resist. Before she made it to the swing doors, she was already coating him in a dark green, viscous film, until his whole body was a glistening, antique bronze, like some ancient Roman hero. With relish she started to lick it off him, her tongue quivering as she savoured the nutty flavour of the oil and the firm, smooth texture of his skin. It was a feast of a very particular kind, and put the smile back on her lips and a peculiar gleam in her eye.

Bruno cocked a questioning eyebrow as she entered.

'Just thinking of something I'd like to try with the pumpkin seed oil.' She tried to sound casual. He wasn't to know it wasn't of a culinary nature. At least she hoped he had no notion of what was going on in her head.

Rosella let the man finish his soup while she discreetly polished cutlery in the background. There was nothing worse than being stared at while you ate. It could ruin a good meal. Besides, she had her own preoccupations. Visions so life-like they seemed to exist. Sensations so physical she couldn't just ignore them.

By the time his bowl was empty, her body was tingling.

And still no one else came in.

Maybe, when things got busier, she'd be able to keep her mind on track.

She uncorked the fruitier Chardonnay. The perfect complement to the guinea fowl breast. More golden in hue than the pale lime of the Riesling, it had sufficient body to accompany the tangier kinds of poultry. A wine that deserved the title 'nectar of the gods'. But Rosella was wise enough not to let scenes of bacchanal frivolity enter her head. She knew where that could lead.

Her mouth watered as she brought in the second course. The sweet, succulent flesh of the guinea fowl on its bed of caramelised vegetables was just begging to be eaten. Like a juicy young thing waiting naked for someone to come and take her. Dreaming of lips planting kisses on her thighs, then working their way up over her stomach to her breasts and pert little nipples.

Rosella felt her own nipples harden at the thought of how those lips would close round the rosy points and begin to suck, pulling gently at a place deeper within her, until tiny spasms began to shoot through her cervix.

Rosella stiffened mid-step as just such a spasm pulsated through her own sex.

She cursed. Things were getting far too real for her own good. But how do you stop your body from responding when your mind has a will of its own? Food and its flavours were her greatest love. Nothing compared in its variety and subtlety.

How she would have liked to pull up a chair beside her guest and share his meal. Pinch mouthfuls from his fork. Steal the very flavours from his lips. A yearning that was hard to keep in check. But such intimacy was out of the question.

Instead, she waited unobtrusively until he'd finished. After she'd taken his plate away, she poured a glass of the Cabernet Sauvignon. As she brought it over to him its blackcurrant aroma filled her nostrils. If it were possible to become inebriated without drinking a sip, then Rosella was already drunk from the thought of its potent, herby flavour.

She made her way to the kitchen, revelling in the carnal pleasure of the rich, red meat to come. A raw, primeval, hedonistic pleasure – like sex itself. And there was nothing to beat Bruno's venison, basted in honey, then steeped in its own juices and crushed coriander. As the heady scent rose from the plate to greet her, Rosella's juices began to flow, too. And not just those in her mouth. She couldn't blame it on the venison. The rogue this time was a Scottish laird, who took her on top of a pile of furs in front of a roaring fire. A man who tasted peaty with good whisky and smelt of bracken and spruce trees. A man whose love-making was as fervent as his passion for hunting. And she was his quarry. He knew no mercy – relentlessly he thrust into her, until her body was a quivering wreck and she was begging him to stop, unable to take any more. A vision that had Rosella burning with desire.

She tried to pull herself together, and concentrated on the baby carrots with a tuft of stalk arranged fan-like on the plate. But her body was trembling and her cervix pulsating from the imaginary battering it had received. Ardour that was getting impossible to conceal. And she was getting hungry, too.

She looking longingly at the gnocchi, made with fresh walnuts Bruno cracked open with his fingers, and chopped with frightening precision.

For a moment Rosella wondered how it would feel to be moulded by those big, warm, dangerous hands. And an ache of want pulsated through her.

She withdrew to behind the bar until her guest had

91

finished the venison, pangs of hunger competing with pangs of need.

'For dessert there's a choice of tiramisù, chestnut sorbet or apple fritters.'

To Rosella there was no contest. Yet the man chose the apple fritters.

Rosella raised her eyebrows in disbelief.

'It's the simple things that mark out a good cook. The best test is an omelette,' he replied dryly.

It seemed a funny kind of criterion for a choice of dessert, but if he wanted to test one, Bruno's omelettes were legendary.

She kicked open the swing doors with more force than was needed and they clattered back to mock her.

Bruno just shrugged when she gave her order.

He peeled and cored an apple, with lightening dexterity, while Rosella bemoaned the lack of guests, and complained about the one they did have. Until her lament was silenced by a kiss, briefly snatched between jobs.

Rosella was so astonished she stood looking at Bruno with her mouth open. He gave another of his infamous grins. Then pulled her towards him.

Their lips met, their tongues intertwined, and for endless seconds they were united in frenzied exploration of each other. It was a kiss like she'd never experienced before. Urgent and insistent, full of pent-up longing. Had they been circling round each other, neither admitting how they yearned for the other?

As they kissed, she could feel every muscle in his body tighten in response. And there was something hard under his apron, jabbing her in the groin. She shivered with excitement. The very object of her rapacious appetite – and crying out to be devoured.

As they broke apart, Bruno looked deep into her eyes, then lifted her onto the worktop. He *could* read her mind.

With one hand he began to dip the rings of apple in batter, while the other caressed her body. His hands seemed to be all over her. Stroking and fondling. Rosella was barely aware of his fumbling with his own trousers, or fiddling with the knobs on the cooker. The sensations overtaking her were too overwhelming.

As the apple rings began to sizzle, Rosella's desire reached sizzling point, too. And Bruno didn't waste a second. He'd pulled down her panties and penetrated before she could grasp it was all really happening.

Love on the fast burner. A stolen moment. Frenetic and furious. And, oh, so real.

But Rosella didn't need any lengthy foreplay. She was more than ready. Her yearning for love had been mounting all evening. Now she succumbed like the butter melting into his caramel sauce. And this was just as rich and sweet. The ultimate enjoyment.

It was better than any of her fantasies. Imagined lovers that were real enough in her head, but who she couldn't hold, or smell, or taste.

With Bruno everything was different. The heat he gave off set her skin burning. His chin grazed her cheeks with its sandpaper roughness, a scouring that made them glow and tingle. The musky scent of his sweat filled her nostrils. And the firmness of his body bruised her tender flesh.

It was just the way it should be.

Real. Physical.

Sex at its most urgent and violent.

Her body soon quaked in the wake of this ramrod battering. Spasms shot through her cervix and her sex began to throb, until she felt it was humming. On the brink of release.

And still it continued.

The force of his thrusts knocked her further and further back on to the worktop. Hot fat spat and crackled just inches from her thigh. And the air was a steamy, suffocating concoction of scents. Yet Rosella wouldn't have swapped it for a feather bed in a big city hotel.

This was love on the wild side. Impetuous. Dangerous. And raging headlong towards its climax.

Then it came. In rippling tides. Wave after wave of pleasure.

A climax that robbed her of her senses and made everything else seem irrelevant.

She hung on to Bruno. Helpless and moaning with ecstasy. Her sex ached from the pouting spasms that gripped it. But she didn't want it to stop. Sex had never been so good.

Abruptly Bruno withdrew as the fritters started to brown. The spasms ebbed away, spluttering to an end as he lifted her from the worktop.

Rosella straightened her clothes and returned to the restaurant. Her lipstick was gone. Yet her lips were still a vibrant red – from the urgent brutality of Bruno's kisses. Wisps of hair fell provocatively into her forehead and stray ringlets curled down over her ears and at the nape of her neck. She looked more gypsy-like than ever. Wild and unrestrained.

If the man noted the transformation, he didn't comment.

Rosella closed the restaurant after a few late guests had gone. It had been a disappointing start. Still, in the kitchen there was Bruno. ...And a whole pan of tiramisù.

She didn't yet know La Zingarella was about to get the best write-up the region's most respected restaurant critic had ever given. A man notoriously difficult to please.

Pubslut
by Emily Dubberley

I'd been seeing Andy for five years. When we met, the sex was amazing but once we got married, it became more sporadic. We both had demanding jobs and active social lives so were often too tired to do anything. I began to lose my confidence, so when my work-colleague Jake started coming on to me, I fell into an affair. It was entirely lust-based and we had no desire to have a proper relationship. It just worked well; he got sex without commitment and I got the attention I desperately needed.

I didn't like lying to Andy and felt incredibly guilty. One night in the pub, after too many drinks, I confessed, terrified it would be the end of the relationship but knowing that Andy was so much more important to me than Jake and I couldn't lie to him any more. I got the shock of my life at his response.

"Do you love me?" he'd asked.

"Yes, more than anything."

"Do you want us to stay together?"

"If you'll still have me."

"Do you still want to fuck Jake?"

"No, I love you..." I started.

He raised his eyebrows and interrupted. "Be honest. If you do, I don't mind. As long as I can have the occasional bit of fun too..."

I imagined Andy fucking another woman and a sting of jealousy went through me. Then I thought of Jake... The way he stroked and kissed every inch of me, taking me to the edge of coming before he plunged his cock in me. His penchant for tying me up and teasing me for hours. The way he always had some dirty surprise; one day Haagen Dazs to be eaten off my body, another some sex toy designed to drive me wild. If I was honest, I could balance out my jealousy if I was allowed to fuck Jake. And it gave me a kick knowing that Jake would think I was being unfaithful, when in fact Andy would know exactly what I was going out to do.

"If you're sure?" I said.

"Good. Mind if I go out on Friday night?"

I knew he was intending to find a woman to fuck and despite the jealousy, felt a mild thrill at the thought of it.

"Okay. I'm sure I'll find something to do..."

The complicit smile that passed between us reminded me of why I'd fallen in lust with him in the first place. "But tonight..." Andy looked me up and down brazenly, "I think you deserve some punishment for what you've done."

Another thrill went through me and I nodded.

"First," he said, looking round at the packed pub, "I want you to go into the toilets. Frig yourself off through your knickers then take them off – you can pass them to me when you come back so I know you've behaved – and they'd better be wet. I want to know you're ready for me to take you whenever I want – and wherever we are."

I blushed, wondering how I'd be able to get away with it. The cubicles were small and there was always a queue. And I'm not the quietest person when I come, even when I masturbate. Andy knew this and wanted to humiliate me. Even worse, my skirt was short and the warm weather meant I was bare-legged.

"I'll be getting hard thinking of you rubbing yourself off

for me with all those other women so close, and walking through the bar with your wet cunt easily reachable for every man in the place," he said.

"Oh, and two other things... Make your fingers nice and wet for me – I want to suck your juices of them when you get back. And..." he grinned, evilly. "Get a round in on your way back."

"But... my fingers will be wet."

"Yes. Let's just hope the barman doesn't notice... Well, what are you waiting for?"

I hurried to the loos to do as I was told.

The toilets were busy as ever so I had to queue for a while, hoping that Andy wouldn't punish me further for the delay. I imagined what he'd do to me and began to feel a familiar warmth.

"Your turn, love." The woman behind me tapped my shoulder and I blushed, realising I'd been lost in sordid reverie.

I went in. As with most pub toilets, the door wouldn't lock. I realised I'd have to lean against the door and hope no one looked underneath to see if it was taken. I braced myself against the door and slid my hand to my cunt. As I started to rub myself, I was surprised to feel how wet I was already. I thought about what Andy would make me do later. Would he fuck me in the pub? Make me suck him off? Make me suck the barman off? Despite my nerves, I could feel the lust surge through me as I envisaged depraved scenarios and was soon coming, biting my lip hard to stop myself from crying out.

Taking my knickers off, and running them over my cunt once more to make sure they were wet enough for him, I stuffed them into my bag. I almost opened the door but remembered his other request just in time. I slid three fingers of my left hand up my cunt and moved them around to get them wet. Hoping like hell the barman wouldn't notice, sure everyone would know what I'd been doing from the smell of sex lingering on me, I headed for the bar.

The barman smiled as I went to the bar. He knows, I thought, before banishing the thought for being paranoid.

"Congratulations," he said.

"Sorry?"

"Your boyfriend – sorry, fiancé told me the good news. Let's see the ring."

Bastard, I thought. Andy knew I'd have made my left hand wet to avoid detection so he'd come up with an excuse to make sure the barman saw it.

"Round's on the house by the way," said the barman.

"Cheers."

"But come on, I know you want to show the ring off."

I thought quickly and curled my hand into a fist, hoping it would hide my secret. "Here you go." I made myself hold my hand out for a few seconds, each one feeling like an age, then grabbed the drinks from the bar and scurried off.

I got back to our table and Andy smiled. "Like the ring, did he?"

"Bastard!"

"Well, if you hadn't let yourself get fucked by another man... And anyway, we've only just begun. Give me your knickers."

I handed them to him under the table and he opened them out and felt them for wetness.

"You are a horny little slut, aren't you. Now let me taste those fingers."

I looked around, hoping no one would notice, and brought my hand to his lips. He sucked my fingers into his mouth, one by one, swirling his tongue round them and sending an erotic tingle through my body.

"I love the way you taste," he said in a husky voice. "If you're very good, you might get to feel my tongue down there later."

Another thrill went through me and I began to wonder at this new side of Andy, almost wishing I'd found it sooner, shocked at this side of me! I removed my fingers from his mouth when he looked at me with permission in his eyes and we sat drinking our pints and making normal conversation, whilst all the time I was getting wet thinking of what would happen next.

"We're leaving," he said, as soon as we finished our beer.

I stood up, eager to know what would happen next. It didn't take long to find out. As soon as we were out of the pub, he dragged me into a side-street and down a quiet alley.

"Get on your knees and suck me," he ordered.

I put my bag down to protect my knees from the ground and knelt on it, knowing that refusing was not an option and secretly aroused at the way he was treating me. I unzipped his fly and pulled his engorged cock from his jeans. I leaned forward and lapped at its salty tip before sucking him into my mouth.

He gripped onto my hair – something he'd never done before – and began fucking my mouth, letting me know that he was the one in control. My naked cunt was dripping and I began to worry that my juices would be visible on my bare thighs when we walked back. "Suck it, you slut," he said, and I worried someone would hear – and if they did, what his response would be. I didn't need to worry. Looking down at me taking his cock all the way down my throat while he fucked my mouth took him over the edge and he shot hot spunk over my tongue, pulling out while it was still spurting from his cock so that I got a faceful of come too.

I went to wipe it off. "Oh no," he said. "You're a cheap slut. You're walking home with my come on your face so that everyone who sees us will know it."

My cheeks burned, but I could feel my juices trickling

down my thighs and knew that my body was responding despite my humiliation.

He deliberately walked home slowly. It was only a five-minute walk but it felt like miles. I could smell his come, feel it running down my face and knew that if anyone saw us, it would be obvious what we'd been doing.

He paused when we got to the shop on the corner of our street. "Do we need any milk? Or maybe cigarettes? Perhaps I should make you get some."

"Please, don't..." I begged.

"Well, maybe not tonight. But I wonder..." He pulled me close to him and slid three fingers up my cunt which twitched involuntarily at the invasion. "Yes, you like the idea. But it's home-time now..." He began to walk, his fingers still up my cunt, leading me down the street.

When we got into the house, he pushed his fingers in my mouth. "Suck your juices off me. I like the idea of you tasting yourself."

I obliged.

"Like that, do you? Maybe..," he pondered, "I'll make you fuck yourself with your dildo and then lick it clean?" He paused, thinking.

"Then again, it might be fun to go back to the pub and get some woman here to fuck in front of you to show you what a bad girl you've been."

He thrust his fingers up me again. "Oh, you really like that idea, don't you. Perhaps I'll make you lick my spunk out of her hole after I've shot it up her?"

Despite myself, my clit twitched at the obscene images he was putting in my head and I began to imagine myself indulging in the depraved acts he was suggesting.

"Actually, no. I'll save that for another time. Tonight I think I'll keep it simple." He pushed me over the table and pushed up my skirt before spreading my legs wide. His

100

finger dipped into my cunt briefly, then probed my arsehole, and I knew what he was thinking. I'd never done it before – always said it was my last taboo – but tonight it seemed only fair. "Yes, I think I'll fuck that tight little arse. Stay there."

He went into the bedroom and came back with some lube. I didn't even know we owned any but clearly he'd wanted to try this for a while... Holding it high over my arse, he dripped it agonisingly slowly over my arse.

I flinched at the cold but when he pulled apart my cheeks and poured it directly into my arsehole, I shuddered in anticipation. He started by slipping in a finger to get me ready, then added more fingers, stretching me wide. It was sore at first but as I got used to the sensation of him frigging my arsehole, I began to feel a dark kind of pleasure. He slipped his thumb round to rub on my throbbing clit and I began to grind against him.

"I think you're ready," he said, his voice little more than a groan. He slid the tip of his cock into my hole and I gasped at the sensation, feeling so stretched, convinced he'd never get it all the way in. I was wrong. He moved slowly at first but as he got deeper into me, he couldn't help thrusting into me – and I liked it!

He grabbed my tits and started pinching my nipples hard. "You love this, you little cheating slut, don't you. You like being treated like the whore you are."

I groaned my assent. At that, he moved a hand down to my cunt and slipped two fingers inside me. Being filled in both holes at once was amazing. I came in seconds, my cunt and arsehole spasming and making him shoot his load up my arsehole. He pulled out and lay on top of me, holding me tight with love.

That was the first time he punished me. And after that, I knew that there was no way I was going to behave myself all the time. The punishment was just too much fun...

Any Three Can Play
by Alex Severn

"Who the hell is that at this time?"

Neither of the couple spoke until the knock came again, louder, more urgent-sounding than the first one. But the look of command in his eyes was too much for her to resist and so it was the woman who went to answer it.

He heard a brief conversation and then the visitor appeared in the living room, looking nervous, hesitant, but more importantly for him, looking gorgeous.

She was a brunette with expensively-cut short hair. She was small in height but the cream-coloured summer dress she was wearing showed enough of her body for him to admire the curves. He could enjoy the way the rain outside had made it a little more transparent and whether her nipples were more visible because the dress was wet or through the drop in temperature that the night had brought, he didn't care. The dress stopped well above her knees and the man gazed openly, almost hungrily at the tanned, shapely legs that tapered into the sandals which were great for a beach, but only when the hot weather blessed it.

"Tom, this lady has broken down. She's had to walk from the main road as she had no money on her mobile. It's okay if she phones the AA from here, isn't it?"

Tom smiled, but somehow the young girl felt it was the smile on the face of the tiger.

103

"Of course she can. But at this time, she could have a long wait for them to come. That's if they ever find this place of course."

Tom turned up the power on the smile as he got up and moved so he was standing close to their visitor's face.

"This place isn't on any maps. It was a farmhouse years ago but only the postman can find it now and if he's on holiday the relief bloke never gets here. You could use the phone if you want to try it?"

The other woman, seemingly more nervous than the visitor said, in a rush of words: "We have a lot of room. Why doesn't she stay here until the morning and then I can drive her to a garage when it's light. That would be all right, wouldn't it, Tom?"

Tom thought for a second.

"Well, if you're desperate for company, Dawn, fine. Sort it out, go on."

It seemed as though the girl had no say in the matter, her fate had been decided for her. Pausing only to find out their guest's name was Emma, Dawn disappeared to get a room habitable for her, leaving Tom and Emma together.

"Do you want a drink, love? A proper one, I mean?"

"Well, maybe I need one after a night like this. You got any vodka?"

When Tom handed her the glass, he lingered close to her, his eyes soon moving down from her face to take in her cleavage, hungrily and without apparent embarrassment. Of course, the way she held his hand a fraction longer than was strictly necessary as she took the vodka didn't do anything to discourage him, and Tom felt her hazel-coloured eyes weigh him up, or was that in his imagination? Perhaps she always licked her lips like that when she drank vodka, perhaps not. Dawn was a stupid tart; okay, he might play a little rough with her now and again and maybe he wasn't the most faithful husband in the world but she was lucky to

104

have him and she ought to be glad of it. Plenty of women looked at him. He knew that he was good-looking. This girl was a good few years younger than him, but so what? Dawn knew who was the boss, both at home and outside and...

"Okay then, Emma, I can show you to your room now."

Her words seemed to break a spell that had been building and as Tom poured himself another whisky, he reluctantly accepted that in the morning she would be gone and the best he would be left with was the fantasy that was already beginning to fill his mind. Yes, when he was away on his business trips he had enjoyed lots of great nights with women who were only too willing, but even a man like him had some limits as to how far he would go, and with Dawn under the same roof...

He almost cried out in his confusion when he felt the hand on his arm but as his vision cleared, he saw her, in her bra and knickers, and her gesture of the need to be silent was unnecessary. The luminous clock told him it was nearly three and with two furtive glances at the obviously fast-asleep Dawn, Tom, naked, followed Emma, quietly closing the bedroom door behind him. He could feel his heart beating faster as the girl went into her room and closed it soundlessly behind both of them. Tom opened his mouth to speak but she placed a finger on his lips and then, almost savagely threw her arms around him, tilting her face to meet his, fastening her soft lips onto his open mouth. As she kissed him he felt a hand caressing his back, sliding down to the base of his spine. His erection was already pushing against her stomach and he had a pang of disappointment as she broke away from him but it didn't last as she pulled off her bra revealing beautifully-shaped breasts, her nipples hardening. Emma licked the fingers on her left hand and began to manipulate her nipples rapidly but the excitement that surged through Tom at the sight of that couldn't begin to prepare him for what happened next. Emma tore off her knickers and plunged her other hand between her legs, stroking, probing, moving her lower body backwards and forwards as if in time with some unheard music. She gasped in pleasure and Tom could see, even from where he was stood, how wet she was, how open her lips were. The tight, thick black curls of hair around her soaking pussy held his gaze completely, he was almost transfixed.

Should he go to her? Should he carry on enjoying the show?

But Emma was in charge, that was clear and suddenly she had turned and almost leapt onto the bed. Sliding up onto all fours with her deliciously shaped bum facing him, she turned her head towards him and whispered, "Take me, take me now."

Tom strode over to her, positioning himself behind her and rammed his hard shaft deep into her, making her almost overbalance with the movement. He placed his hands on her back lightly as he began to build a rhythm of thrusting and driving but soon he found his hands further forward, his fingers around each nipple; he had never known a woman whose nipples could harden so much. He felt she was almost collapsing with the power of him inside her and, somewhat reluctantly he moved his hands to grasp her around her thighs and, making sure it didn't spoil the incredible feeling of the way they had been joined together, he lifted her legs upwards. She let out a moan so loud he was afraid it would wake Dawn but nothing really mattered now but this moment and as her face fell forward until she was almost kissing the pillow, he adjusted her body so that he was driving down into her from an angle he had never imagined. Praying he could keep going he felt her lips tighten around him, it was almost as if she was coaxing him to be bigger and harder, as if her saturated, bloated lips were talking him into her body. Then, it was over. He surged into her, the throbbing went right through his system as they both collapsed onto the bed, gasping for breath.

Breakfast was a very strange affair, how could it be anything else? Not for the first time, Tom congratulated himself on having no scruples and no conscience. Of course, he could leave Dawn and he would have plenty of other women who would want him but it was convenient for him to stay with her, enjoying her now and again, and anyway she was clearly happy to let him treat her like he did, wasn't she? Some women liked to be treated badly, it turned them on. Her cooking was getting worse though, those sausages tasted terrible. Perhaps they could afford a housekeeper.

Funny though, the way Dawn was looking at Emma, it was almost as if she knew and was okay with that. Now that really was weird, unless... It was there in the magazines and on the porn films he'd seen often enough. Perhaps a threesome was exactly what Dawn was after, maybe sharing him with another woman was her fantasy. Emma was still flirting with him, not bothering to wait until Dawn had turned her back to make another pot of tea? And then she uncrossed her legs, nice and slow and, my God, she wasn't wearing anything under that dress! Emma licked her lips as she gazed at him, making all of the memories of last night leap back into his mind but he instinctively turned to make sure Dawn wasn't watching, but actually she was, and she'd found time to strip off her clothes as well.

Tom's eyes flashed between the two women, Emma now standing and laughing softly as she peeled off her dress and Dawn, a few feet away from her, her shaved, blonde pussy seeming more inviting to him than he could ever remember. He felt Dawn unbutton his shirt and start to massage his chest, which had already started sweating, but his temperature started to rocket as he saw her move behind

107

Dawn and fondle her boobs vigorously. With a very girlish giggle, Dawn broke away from Tom completely and the two women fell into each others' arms, their bodies jammed together. Then, easing away from each other, Tom saw his wildest fantasy begin to come true as the women fell onto the ground in a heap.

He saw Emma's fingers reach out and stroke the erect bud of Dawn's swollen clitoris, almost felt the surge of pleasure it sent through her. Then, he gasped as Dawn hastily pushed Emma's hand away from her lips as she had been pleasuring herself and replaced them with her own mouth, licking and probing with her tongue, making the brunette writhe with pleasure. He felt his cock stiffen inside his jeans. He was ready to join them but this was so wild, seeing them rolling around as if he wasn't there to watch them. By now Emma's mouth was returning the favour to Dawn. Tom's heart was pounding faster; he had a ringside seat as he watched Emma's tongue coax more and more dampness from her playmate's mouth. He knew he was seconds away from being the central character in the best porn film ever made. He imagined Emma's lively and flexible tongue licking the tip of his shaft, could almost feel her mouth clamping shut over the huge width of his cock... That was the last thing he remembered.

Tom's head felt like lead, the slightest movement sent spasms of pain scything through his temples. The light hurt his eyes but gradually he began to adjust to the atmosphere. Why was he lying in the spare bedroom, he must get up and...as he moved his body forward, he was yanked backwards. He was tied up, naked, both hands behind him. A prisoner. What had happened – burglars? Burglars must have come and... Emma, was she okay? Oh and Dawn as well, poor cow, where were they?

But soon, he had the answer.

They were dressed quite sensibly for the time of year. It

108

hadn't been a hot summer and the suitcases told him they might be going a long way. North, south, they seemed flexible on that.

But he had to concentrate hard on what Dawn was saying, his head was still spinning.

"I actually thought you might be suspicious, you know, sexy young bird arrives, flirts with you almost in front of me and then screws you in the next room, but I should have guessed when you're as conceited as you are it would seem natural. How could any woman resist you, eh? Well, we'll manage to. Sorry about the drug, it'll wear off. I can't untie you because I don't trust you, you might get rough and keep me here. I'll phone someone up tomorrow, they'll have a good laugh at you lying there naked but it won't hurt you to suffer a bit. Glad you enjoyed our show but for the record, we both like men as well. It's just that Emma taught me lots of things, this was her idea actually. To think, if I hadn't met her at that party when you were away yet again, I might still be waiting on you while you were sleeping with anything with a pulse.

Well. It's been fun, Tom... Actually, it's been rubbish, but it's over now."

Dawn reached forward and ran her hands over his limp cock, smiling as, despite his anger, he started to become aroused.

"There, that's to keep you going until tomorrow."

They hade gone before he had a chance to speak but then, really, he couldn't think of anything to say.

One November Evening
by Katie Lilly

He was standing at the far side of the bedroom, with his back towards her, his tanned skin glistening with perspiration as he ran his hand through his dark, damp hair. It was the first chance she'd had to really look at him and she let her eyes stray over his naked body. He was around six feet tall with long legs and well-defined thighs. His arms betrayed a similar athleticism and she wondered how many days a week he worked out.

She remained in bed, lying on her back with her legs bent at the knees forming snowy white peaks in the duvet. She watched as he reached down and retrieved his briefs from the bedroom floor and, as he did so, she caught a glimpse of his now flaccid cock. He continued to get dressed while she watched from the bed.

It was a typical November evening – dark and cold, with a fine drizzle in the air, when Lucy spotted him at the bus stop. She was waiting for the traffic lights to turn green and his black-clad body was moving under the golden glow of the street lamp as he stamped his feet to keep warm. The light illuminated his face and revealed a Roman nose, thin lips, sturdy chin and dark brows to match his dark-coloured hair. His tight, black jeans betrayed only a hint of the lean, firm body underneath.

Lucy was on her way home from an evening out with work colleagues. She had only been with the company a little over a year and, thrilled with her recent promotion, was happy for the chance to celebrate. As work was the main thing the women had in common, conversation inevitably turned to the latest office gossip. Lucy learned that David from Accounts was single again and Rebecca was moving to Australia. As much as she enjoyed the evening, after six orange juices she was ready to go home to the bottle of red wine she had waiting.

She had hardly recognised Christopher, who wore a suit at work, shivering at the bus stop in his jeans and T-shirt. He worked with David, but their office was based at a sub branch, two miles from head office. He had only been with the company a couple of months and Lucy had seen him just once at an equality and diversity training day.

As the lights turned green she pulled alongside the bus stop, wound down the passenger window and shouted, "Christopher, do you need a lift? … hey … Christopher … Chris." He stared at her for a moment, so she waved, gesturing for him to get in the car and he finally responded, climbing into the passenger seat.

"You must be freezing in that T-shirt – have you been waiting long?" she said, turning up the heating as she pulled away from the kerb. "Over half an hour – thanks for the lift," he shivered as he tried to get warm, "Where are we heading?"

After a moment's thought, Lucy said, "Why don't you come to my house for a night cap – I left some wine breathing before I went out and the house should be warm as the central heating is on?"

"Sounds good," he replied.

The journey from the bus stop to Lucy's house took no more than ten minutes and she did most of the talking. They soon found themselves sitting on Lucy's sofa, drinking wine and listening to 'late night love' on the radio.

As if sensing her gaze upon him, he turned and with three large, confident strides was alongside the bed. She lowered her legs and he sat down on the bed's edge, facing her, his lower body dressed in black jeans. With the duvet between her naked body and his bare chest, he bent forward and placed his lips firmly on hers, with a passion and energy which surprised her. She parted her lips and pushed her tongue into the soft, wet recess of his mouth, running her hand through his hair and holding him firmly in position. He responded, playfully flicking his tongue from one side of her mouth to the other.

Lucy closed her eyes and allowed herself to be absorbed by his kiss. She felt as if her whole body was engulfed by this man and a wave of loss swept over her as he gently pulled back. She eased her hold on him and slid her hand along the downy nape of his neck and back to her side. He was still leaning over her but as she reached forward, her mouth seeking to be reunited with his, he put his hand firmly on her shoulder, holding her down in the soft bedding.

He took hold of the top edge of the duvet and pulled it down to her waist, revealing the soft peaks of her breasts. Reaching forward he pressed his lips firmly to her right breast and began to work her growing, pink nipple, circling round and round with his tongue. He then clamped his lips around it like a rock-pool limpet and sucked hard. As he sucked he occasionally allowed his teeth to catch the edge of the hard nipple and every time he did so, Lucy gasped with pain and pleasure. While attending to this breast with his mouth he reached over with his hand and, using his index finger, mirrored the circling motion of his tongue around the other nipple.

Lucy's breasts began to tingle with delight at the sensations his lips and fingers were arousing. Her breath

113

quickened and the delight spread down her body to the heat now rising between her legs. She could already feel herself getting wet as her body responded in excited expectation. She parted her legs a little, frustrated that they were trapped under the weight of the duvet. As she tried to wriggle her legs wider apart, he lifted his mouth from her breast and went back to her soft, tender lips.

They had been sitting on the sofa in her living room the first time she felt his lips on hers. She was sat next to him, with her legs up underneath her, so they were facing each other. They were only half way down their first glass of wine when he reached forward and kissed her. His kiss was gentle, almost chaste and she tasted the red wine on his lips.

It hadn't taken long for the first kiss to lead to another and, as they finished a second glass of wine, his hand was underneath her top, rubbing her breasts through the shiny silk fabric of her bra. She responded by stroking his jean-clad thigh and occasionally allowing her hand to brush up against his groin. She could feel his cock hardening under her fingers and his body responded, gently thrusting out towards her hand.

Lucy hadn't quite known where her offer of a lift would take them and this was certainly leading to more than she had bargained for, but she was enjoying herself and she offered no resistance as he reached around her back to unclip her bra. He fumbled with the clasp a little but then her breasts were released and he pushed up her top and bra to view his accomplishment. Restricted by the clothing now around her neck, she pulled the fabric over her head to reveal her naked chest.

Lucy carefully unbuckled the belt on his jeans and slid the zip down slowly. Reaching inside she could feel his erection and his cock easily slipped out of his briefs and into her hand. He shifted his bodyweight and tugged his jeans lower to reveal a mass of dark curly hair at the base of the shaft. Holding his cock in her hand, Lucy bent forward and flicked her tongue around the head and then ran it along the shaft and back up to the head. She opened her mouth and guided him inside so she could taste him. He responded with a groan and a pelvic thrust, putting him deeper inside her mouth. Moving in rhythm to his thrusts Lucy's mouth slid up and down the shaft of his cock, as she worked to bring him to orgasm – her bare breasts bouncing on his thigh. His hardness filled her mouth as she consumed as much of him as she could. After a few moments she felt the caution of his hand on her shoulder. She lifted her head, and placed his cock between her breasts, for the last couple of thrusts and the release of his warm, milky ejaculate.

He tucked his cock back into his briefs almost as soon as he'd come and zipped up his jeans. Lucy took her top from the floor and pulled it over her head, rubbing her chest to absorb the liquid deposit he'd left her. She poured the last of the wine into their glasses and started a conversation about the song, now playing on the radio. As he finished the last of his wine, he stood up and Lucy thought this signalled an end to their evening. She was taken aback when, at the front door, he reached out his hand and led her upstairs to her bedroom.

The kiss lasted only a moment this time as he pulled away and stood up. He looked at her face and glanced over her naked breasts before returning to her face. Lucy's body was alive and she wanted satisfaction. She reached forward, slid her hand along his upper thigh and rubbed his groin with the back of her hand. He smiled, but she could feel no other response from under the heavy denim of his jeans. For a moment she considered sliding down the zip but then she had another idea.

The duvet was now free from the weight of his body and

she kicked it off to one side to reveal her full nakedness. In a single motion she spread her legs and bent them at the knee, offering up her cunt for his inspection. She reached down with her right hand and teasingly entangled her fingers in her pubic curls. She looked up at his face, to make sure he was watching and began to rub over her clitoris, her fingers in a slow rhythmic dance. With her left hand she reached up, cupped her breast and using her thumb around the nipple, matched the erotic dance below.

She watched him, transfixed by her action, his gaze on her hand and the rhythmic rubbing on her clit. She smiled and, enjoying the audience, moved her fingers into the wet softness inside, before lifting her fingers to her mouth to taste her own desire. She then reached into the sweetness again and this time held up her hand to offer him the delicacy. He knelt by the side of the bed as he reached forward, guiding her fingers to his mouth. He licked her fingers as if taking honey from a spoon and then devoured them whole, sucking hard to get every last drop. Her body was still throbbing to the tune of the dance, although it was no longer receiving attention and Lucy longed to quench the desire within her.

She reached over to her bedside table and, pulling out a drawer, removed a long, phallic-shaped blue vibrator. Resuming her previous position she took the substitute cock in her right hand, flicked it on and guided it between her legs. As she was already aroused it slid easily inside her and the vibrating sensations shot through her body. As she moved the vibrator in and out, mimicking the action of a man, she increased the intensity by turning the end of the vibrator. She didn't care now whether he was watching or not as she only wanted to satisfy the need growing within her.

He was still kneeling on the floor but had moved to the foot of the bed and was staring directly at the action between her legs. He reached out and, placing his hands on her knees, gently pushed her legs wider apart. Then he began to caress the insides of her thighs, running his fingers from her knees to her curls and back again, over and over. Her breathing quickened and she began to moan gently with every breath out.

She felt his hand on the vibrator and she let go, surrendering control of the sex toy. He was tentative at first, sliding the long piece of rubber inside her slowly and keeping the thrusts shallow but, as his confidence grew, he increased the intensity and soon he was penetrating deeply into her cunt. Her soft, wet flesh enveloped almost the whole length of the toy and Lucy's moans of pleasure filled the room.

She knew she was close to achieving her goal and moved her fingers to her clitoris, resuming the rhythmic dance she began earlier. With expert precision she rubbed over her clit and shouted out as the warm rush of an orgasm engulfed her. Her body quivered and her pelvic muscles gripped the blue phallus as she closed her legs to keep the vibrator in place and prolong the pulsing sensation inside her.

As her body slowly relaxed she let her legs fall open and withdrew the vibrator, rolling onto her stomach and placing the toy on the floor. She remained in that position with her bare arse facing him.

Chris had been on his way home when she'd pulled up at the bus stop. He didn't recognise Lucy but she seemed to know him. He was grateful to be somewhere warm plus she was gorgeous with her long brown hair and brown eyes. He had begun to get aroused the first time they kissed and couldn't resist touching her, but tried not to get too hopeful. Once he felt her at the zip of his jeans however, he could no longer contain himself. Within seconds he'd got his cock in her mouth and was filling her face, thrusting deeply inside. He couldn't hold back for long and all too soon he had come and it was over. He was just about to leave when he felt a familiar flicker in his jeans and thought he'd try his luck – leading Lucy away from the front door and up the stairs.

He was soon bent over her, licking, sucking and fondling to give her pleasure and to give his body time to regenerate but once he felt his cock harden again he was keen for more. With swift, decisive, movements, as regular as a drumbeat, he fucked Lucy in missionary position style. He could feel her respond as she lifted her pelvis up to meet his thrusts and soon his body shuddered as he climaxed inside her. Chris was satisfied, it had been a good fuck and he now got dressed, facing away from Lucy to hide his spent manhood. This time he thought, "I really must go home" but one look back at her and they were soon sharing the passionate kiss which had led them to this moment.

Chris was really aroused watching Lucy fuck herself with the vibrator and now had another erection. With Lucy still lying on her stomach he slipped out of his jeans and briefs and climbed up onto the bed. He sat with his legs astride hers and, starting with her shoulders, gently moved his hands over her warm flesh. Moving down her spine and across her back he let his fingers tease the sides of her breasts before he continued his journey down to reach the cheeks of her arse. He took hold of his cock and, as he playfully tapped his hardness against her skin, Lucy giggled lightly from the folds of the pillow.

"Come up on all fours for me" he said as he moved his weight off her legs to enable Lucy to respond. He was now kneeling up against her body and, as he eased her legs a little wider apart, he guided his cock in between. With a firm grip on her hips he pulled her closer to his body and thrust deep inside a few times before pulling out his cock

118

and wiping it across her arse, leaving a snail trail of moisture. Still holding her hip with his left hand, he used his fingers to gently rub the moisture around her anus and slid his fingers inside. As he explored her delicate hole Lucy began to thrust towards him, following a steady rhythm. A few moments later when Chris replaced his fingers with his hard cock, he felt her body quiver before she continued the rhythm, now pushing her arse onto his manhood.

Chris could feel the different sensation immediately as the tightness sucked in his cock and held it in a vice-like grip. He kept his hands on Lucy's hips as he guided the full length of his shaft slowly in and out of her arse. He looked down at their joined bodies and felt an excitement mount inside him. As he quickened the pace he could hear the flap, flap of his balls against her arse competing with the slap, slap of Lucy's dangling breasts. Letting go of her hips he leaned forward to silence her breasts, taking one in each hand and flicking the nipples with his thumbs.

As his climax grew, Chris could feel the sweat running down his back. He closed his eyes and the amazing flashes of coloured lights dancing across his eyelids signalled that he was going to come. He returned his hands to Lucy's hips and controlled the pace of the final few thrusts. Keeping his eyes closed, he opened his mouth to get more air into his lungs. As the sensation reached full intensity he let out a groan and filled her hole with his essence. Exhausted and completely spent he slowly withdrew from her body.

The last couple of hours had been a whirl of high intensity which he wouldn't forget. He was now ready to go home and quickly got dressed without glancing once at Lucy. She showed him to the door, where he kissed her briefly on the lips and they said their goodbyes. She didn't ask for his number, so he didn't offer it. He glanced back once as he walked down the path and saw her wave, as she tried to hide her naked body behind the door.

It had been two weeks since Lucy's 'big night out' or to be more accurate, her 'big night in'. She had been trying to find a reason to go over to the sub branch building where Christopher worked but she had been too busy since her promotion. This afternoon however, he was expected at head office for a meeting. As Lucy looked in the mirror she smiled and felt the slight tug of anticipation between her legs at the thought of seeing him again.

Leaving the ladies toilet she headed for the Board Room. As she opened the door she quickly scanned around and her heart rate quickened as she saw him seated at the far end of the room. She smiled in his direction but felt herself getting warm and her skin flushed, so she looked away. Her body was tingling with anticipation and Lucy could sense the wetness developing between her legs.

The meeting began and, anxious to see him, she took a deep breath and looked up again just as he stood up to be introduced to the group. The man standing in front of her was about six feet tall with dark hair and tanned skin but, as he spoke, she looked more closely. His nose was not quite as she remembered and his lips seemed red and thick. As he sat down he looked directly at her and she realised her mistake – this was a stranger.

Her head awash with thoughts, Lucy escaped to the sanctuary of the ladies toilets during the coffee break. Locked inside a cubicle she sat on the toilet with the seat down and put her head in her hands. "What have I done?" she whispered to herself as she thought about the evening a couple of weeks ago. "I only offered him a lift because I thought it was Christopher. I have no idea who I fucked and I didn't even get a phone number because I thought we could get in touch through work."

Getting ready to go back into the meeting Lucy took a

deep breath and decided to focus on the positive. She had enjoyed the sexual liaison immensely and it was a passionate evening which she would always remember. As she walked back into the Board Room she glanced over at the real Christopher. He looked up and, as he smiled, Lucy felt her breasts start to tingle.

Something Natural
by Jean Roberta

My girlfriend, Fennel, was still breathing hard when I worked up the courage to ask her a question. "Why were you so rough that time?" I wondered aloud. I was glad we were in the dark so she couldn't see me blushing. I blush easily.

"Was I rough?" She playfully tweaked one of my nipples, pulling me closer.

"Well, not exactly rough," I stammered. "I mean, I'm not complaining, but…"

"Daisy," she interrupted, "you seemed to want it. So I gave it to you."

My breath caught in my throat, and I didn't trust myself to speak.

"Didn't you?" she persisted.

"Yes," I admitted, almost whispering. "I wanted it. I'm not blaming you, honey, but I don't really think we should…"

I could feel a laugh rippling through her generous body. "Are you telling me you really don't want it?" she demanded, "or you don't think it's politically correct for a lesbian feminist to fuck another lesbian feminist with enthusiasm?"

She had taken the wind out of my sails, as usual. I laughed ruefully. "Well, I guess," I answered vaguely. "I'm just wondering where this kind of thing might lead."

She had already begun to massage my small breasts because she knew I found it hard to refuse her anything when she was doing that. "Where do you think it might lead?" she asked slyly.

"Mm, I can't think, Fennel," I complained.

She laughed, throwing one of her legs over mine. Suddenly she was lying on top of me, her large, soft breasts against mine, her wet crotch against mine, one of her knees nudging my legs apart. "What if I want it again?" she teased. "What if I do it rough? Will you push me away and never speak to me again?"

She was rocking me back and forth in a way she knew I liked. "No," I moaned. I had come hard only minutes before but I was ready for her again. "I can't resist you, Fennel," I admitted, loving the feel of her soft but heavy flesh on mine. "You get to me." Despite my growing arousal, I felt it was important to put my thoughts into words. "But I don't want to be at anyone's mercy," I wailed quietly. "Even yours. I don't want to be controlled. I have a will of my own, you know."

"I know, baby," she murmured soothingly. She clamped her mouth on one of my nipples as her fingers teased my sensitive clit by dipping into my wetness and spreading it around. Her skilful fingers, artisan's fingers, began to manoeuvre within my inner lips, lazily touching and exploring. "You're so wet," she laughed. "I can stop doing this if you like," she offered politely, "so you can dry out."

"No!" I protested, making her laugh again. Her fingers circled near the opening of my pussy as she rocked me back and forth, back and forth.

"Shall I go deeper?" she murmured. "Shall I fuck you, even if it takes us both straight to hell? Do you want it?"

"Yes," I moaned, too excited to slow down. "Please, honey," I begged. "Please do it."

Two eager fingers immediately plunged into my depths, driving me wild. A third finger sneaked partway into me as my hungry lower mouth squeezed and squeezed without any prompting from my brain. She pumped in time to my squeezing until I yelped and squealed in orgasm, holding her in my arms. I knew then that she had a point, but I couldn't guess what she was planning to do with it.

As soon as I felt we were both calm enough to converse rationally, I tried to bring some democracy into our relationship. "Honey, we'd be more equal if you'd let me fuck you, too," I explained. "I'd love to."

"But I'm not into it, Daisy," she insisted. "Maybe I have a psychological block about penetration, but I really don't like it. I enjoy what you do," she told me, referring to my gentle sucking of her easily-excited clit.

"Are you sure that's enough?"

"You should know that," she laughed.

I had no reason not to believe her, judging from the strength of her orgasms, but I was still vaguely dissatisfied.

We were sitting on her thick carpet, gulping Coke to quench our post-sexual thirst.

Fennel's lush curves reminded me of a French Impressionist painting, although her hair, brush-cut and dyed an artificial-looking colour called 'raisin', hardly suggested that period. On her classically beautiful face, she still wore vestiges of black eyeliner and burgundy lipstick. She would have been lovely without makeup, but Fennel could never resist decorating herself; she also had a tattooed rose on one shoulder and a little dragon on one breast. I sometimes accused her of being too easily influenced by passing styles.

She often advised me to quit bitching, hang loose, and go with the flow.

She was looking at my wavy, shoulder-length brown hair, which she was encouraging me to grow long. "It's getting there," she approved, running a hand through it. I couldn't help shivering in response to her touch. My slim, pale body is completely unmarked, and I am proud of its natural grace. I noticed that I was covered with a thin film of sweat, which made my skin shimmer softly. Fennel watched me thoughtfully.

"Daisy," she said, "did I ever tell you I was the femme when I was with Rita?"

"Really?" I asked. "Did you let her fuck you?" I demanded jealously before I could stop myself.

"No," she laughed. she looked both amused and embarrassed. "I let her do other things, though. She liked me to wear a dress when we went out in public, so I did. I wanted to please her – at least, at first." She paused. "I didn't always think of myself as the femme, mind you," she pointed out, "but she liked to think she was the butch." I pictured our friend Rita in her favourite cowboy boots and suede jacket, and saw the truth in Fennel's observation. "What I'm saying, Daisy," she explained, "is that a relationship is a two-way street." I groaned at the cliché. "Sometimes I do things because you seem to want them, and I just can't resist."

She slid closer to me, rubbing one of her breasts against my shoulder. "You're such a cuddly little thing," she chuckled. I turned halfway so I could hold her heavy breasts in my hands. I bent my head to give each of her nipples a quick suck, then came up again to admire her blue-green eyes.

"Fennel, I'm crazy about you," I confessed, "in spite of your faults. I suppose that's why I'm scared."

"That I'll hurt you?" she asked softly.

"Maybe without meaning to."

"Well," she said slowly, "that's the only way it would ever happen, honey. All I can say is I try to give my woman what she wants." She turned around and pulled me against her breasts so that I was cushioned by her body.

"I know," I told her. I had a lump in my throat. "You do that, honey." She kissed the top of my head.

Fennel had been after me for a month to let her use a dildo on me before I finally agreed to it as an experiment. It turned out to be a hard, pink plastic strap-on device that was shaped, to my horror, exactly like a man's cock. Because I had already agreed, I gamely spread my legs and tried to pretend I didn't feel like a rape victim as Fennel began to pump. "Do you like this?" she asked cautiously, already knowing the answer.

"No. I like your tongue and your fingers, Fennel. This isn't the same. I don't want an artificial man." She slowly withdrew from me. I couldn't tell from her expression whether she was disappointed. "I'm sorry," I mumbled.

"It's all right, chick," she assured me. She sometimes called me that to provoke me. I was too apologetic to react.

"How was it for you?" I persisted, wanting to know.

"You weren't opening for me the way you usually do," she said softly, running a hand over one of my breasts. The nipple immediately hardened. "I can't enjoy it if you don't want it," she explained. "It's kind of a chemical reaction. If the ingredients aren't all there, it won't fizz."

I knew she was right, but I also knew that she could make me fizz anytime, any where, without using something that wasn't part of her body.

"I'm not into sex toys," I told her. "I don't need them."

Fennel continued to play with my breasts, but she was obviously distracted. "You like being filled inside," she reminded me. I squirmed from embarrassment as well as from the waves of sensation she was wringing from my nipples. "I can't believe you never masturbated with anything," she said bluntly.

I was overwhelmed by a rush of memories. How had she ever guessed what I used to do with the handle of the bath

127

brush? Or the perfume flask, so conveniently shaped? Or even (at a pinch) candles or the necks of pop bottles?

Fennel's expressive face watched me with interest. "You did!" she announced. "Tell me, bad girl, what did you use?"

"Whatever came to hand," I admitted, feeling foolish but also aroused. "But I think I would have felt too self-conscious using something that was made for that purpose. So I looked for objects of the right size. You know, it had to seem natural and spontaneous. And if my parents ever found that stuff lying around my room, they would never guess." I wrapped my arms around Fennel, feeling her laugh.

"Do you want me to go see if there's a nice, thick vegetable in the fridge?" she teased me.

"No," I told her seriously, "because I don't want you to get out of bed." I began kissing my way down her midriff and belly, then into her jungle of hair. When I got to her hard, little clit, I knew what she wanted. I feasted on her centre of pleasure until her gasps and moans told me I had brought her enough pleasure for the time being.

About a week after that episode, she brought out her surprise. She had massaged my back for awhile, but her hands had slipped down and she was kneading the firm cheeks of my bottom. "I'd like to spank you sometime," she said casually, as if to herself. "you have such a good ass for it." She laughed as I stiffened in alarm. "Don't worry, chick," she assured me. "I won't do it unless you need it. If you're bad."

Without warning, she reached down and pulled an object out from under the bed. I sat up to look at it and waited for Fennel to explain to me what it was. "Something natural," she explained. "Good, wholesome wood." The thing was bigger than an old-fashioned darning egg and smaller than a wooden potato masher. One end was clearly a handle, while the rest was carved in interesting bumps, knobs and swirls.

The whole thing was painted bright red and heavily shellacked.

"What is it for?" I asked.

"What do you think?" she grinned.

I squawked. "Fennel, did you actually make this in your shop just for–"

"Just for you," she assured me. "It looks pretty too, don't you think? And it doesn't resemble any man on this planet. You should thank me."

I had to admire her skill at working with wood. Not to mention working with my flesh and my mind. I wondered what the thing would feel like, and I realised that the knobs and bumps were there to arouse my curiosity before arousing the rest of me. "You're crazy, Fennel," I laughed. She pressed me down on the bed, kissing me with her soft, full lips. Her tongue found its way into my mouth, where it probed my tongue and palate, as eager and inventive as Fennel herself. I moaned in surrender, knowing that I wanted her to fill all the openings in my body and my life. I pulled her close.

She began her usual rocking rhythm. My pussy began to spurt hot juices in response.

"Oh mama," she whispered in a sultry low voice. "This feels good. I'm not gonna let you up for awhile." She pinched my nipples, gently at first, then harder to make me groan.

I stroked her smooth back, loving the feel of her. "Honey," I told her on impulse, "you can do anything to me."

"Anything?" she asked with raised eyebrows, grinning. "Watch out, baby. Here come the ropes and nipple clamps. Maybe a riding crop. "She never broke rhythm as she sucked and lightly bit each of my nipples. "You like that, don't you?" she laughed.

"You're easy to please, sleazy thing." Her gifted mouth

129

worked its way down to my hard, expectant clit. I moaned loudly when she seized it gently between her teeth and began sucking hard.

"Oh, baby," I gasped.

She lifted her head from my hot, wet crotch. "Don't come yet," she warned me. "I'll punish you if you do. You're going to get something else tonight." Her blue eyes glittered.

"Get up," she ordered, pulling me up by the waist. She positioned me on all fours, doggy-style. She bent over my projecting ass, tickling my cunt from behind. She quickly explored my wetness with her fingers, pulling me backward with her other hand.

"Fennel," I moaned, "I want you." She was rocking me backward and forward. The smooth wooden object nudged the opening of my throbbing hole. I could already feel an orgasm building in my aroused clit.

I thought I would stop breathing when Fennel pulled me backward onto her wooden tool, simultaneously pushing and twisting it into me. Its odd surface rubbed and tickled all the folds inside me that had longed to be touched. I squirmed in ecstasy as she pressed herself against me, urging me on. "You love that, don't you, baby?" she crooned, keeping pace with my bucking. "I knew you would. You're such a hot, little bitch." My pussy gulped and clutched at the object that probed it unmercifully.

"Fennel," I gasped urgently, wanting her permission.

"Come now, honey," she urged me. "You can come." The noises from my mouth filled the room as I shook, squeezed and danced around the hard device buried between my thighs. When Fennel slowly, reverently pulled it out, it was covered with liquid.

I lay on my side, pressed into Fennel, as my breathing and my heartbeat subsided into their normal pace. "It's a weird thing," I said shyly, "but it works." She stroked my

130

hair. "I want you to use your designer dildo on yourself," I said suddenly. Fennel jerked in surprise, but I could sense that she was pleased with my suggestion. "You could even do it alone," I offered, "but once you're used to it, I want to watch. Then I could do it to you."

I could feel her warm flesh beginning to yield. After all, she's a generous woman and she knew it was my turn. The mere thought of that red, shiny wooden object disappearing into her wet, swollen cunt excited me. I knew she was intrigued. I turned around so I could hold her, and she relaxed into my slim body.

"Oh yes, chick," she sighed with pleasure. "Please be patient with me. I'm not used to it."

"But you will be, honey." My fingers slid lazily down the crack of her ass to her sopping wet hair and the opening beneath. "There's so much I want to do with you, crazy woman," I told her, realising the truth of it as I said it.

"Oh," she groaned happily, pushing against her fingers. "You're my woman for life, Daisy." I answered her with a kiss that grew more demanding as she melted into it. I knew we would be playing with each other for a long time to come. Naturally.

Bait & Switch
by Landon Dixon

I pulled up to the curb in front of the lingerie store, turned off the car, and took a deep breath. It was only a routine sales stop – to drop off the latest line of lingerie my company was peddling – but this time I'd resolved to finally make a play for Gillian, the busty, forty-something babe who ran the small store. I'd tried to strike up a rapport with her in the past, but had always gotten the cold shoulder instead of the hot breast.

I got out of the car, pulled an assortment of thongs, push-up bras, teddies, and other erotic bedroom garments out of the trunk, and determinedly pushed the door to the store open. A bell rang overhead, announcing my arrival, and the start, and end, of my mission. Gillian wasn't there!

"Hi," I said dejectedly, to the young woman at the cash register. I knew that Gillian's store wasn't big enough for two people to ever be working there at once.

"Hi back at you," the girl said, smiling.

The store was empty of customers, which wasn't unusual for a Monday morning. I walked up to the girl and was about to enquire about my over-ripe Gillian when it finally hit me that the young woman was also gorgeous. It usually took me less than a tenth of a second to pick up on that sort of thing. Thoughts of Gillian faded away like the morning mist – replaced by the soft, hot reality of the sales clerk.

She was maybe twenty. Maybe. And she had long, brown, silky hair that shone under the fluorescent lights. Her eyes were brown, as well, while her lips were red and full and wet-looking. Her skin was the colour of creamed coffee, and she looked like she had some Spanish blood in her. But what really put the wind back in my sails was her burgeoning bosom. If I knew my bra sizes – and being in the women's frilly underwear business, I knew my bra sizes – she was a 38 DD, at least. But she wasn't wearing a bra. Her huge tits were loosely and barely covered by a light green halter top that spelled cleavage with capital letters and a couple of exclamation points.

She looked at the stuff I'd forgot I was carrying and asked, "Are you Mark Hull, by any chance?"

I stared at her overfull, brown tits and nodded vaguely. "Uh, yeah. That's me. How'd you know?"

She laughed. "Gillian told me that you'd be stopping by this morning. I'm Francesca."

I gave my head a shake and reluctantly raised my eyes to hers. "Oh, hi, Francesca," I mumbled. "Um, should I just leave this stuff with you, then?" I held up the lingerie and shrugged.

"Aren't you supposed to gimme a sales pitch or something?"

"Uh, yeah, I guess so. Sure." I cleared my throat. "Well, we've got some new–"

"Not here," she interrupted. "In back. You can set all of that junk down in the storage room and give your arms a rest. Okay? I'll show you." She bounded out from behind the cash register and bounced off towards the rear of the store.

It wasn't the store's rear that interested me at that moment, however, it was Francesca's. Her big, round butt cheeks jiggled playfully within the thin, tan confines of her stretch pants. The girl was an absolute knock-out coming

134

and going. I kept my astonished eyes glued to her trembling ass as I stumbled after her.

We ended up together in a tiny storage room that was the conclusion to a short hallway which veered off to the right at the back of the store.

"Just put your stuff on the counter," Francesca said, indicating with her small hand about a square foot of space that wasn't cluttered with sexy underwear and sales slips, on the counter that ran the length of one side of the narrow room. Lingerie on hangers formed the opposite side of the room. It was a tight squeeze – like the golden space between Francesca's dewy, young breasts where my cock would just barely fit.

I felt the blood flowing from my head to my crotch as my thoughts turned decidedly un-business-like. I set the articles of unclothing down and turned around to find myself bumper to bumper with Francesca. She had the clear advantage in size. "Not much room in here, is there?" I said softly, again ogling the girl's burnished breasts.

"Oh, I don't know," she mused, coyly placing a finger against her pouty lips. "I think the room is just about right."

I smiled uncertainly, then sighed and mentally squared everything away for my sales pitch. But before I could bore her with that, she stood up on her tip-toes and kissed me on the mouth.

My cock made a frantic jump to fullness inside of my pants, helped in no small measure by Francesca's warm hand pressing against it. I gulped in surprise. Everything seemed to suddenly get hot and heavy and humid, and time slowed down to a crawl, and the world shrunk down to just me and the Latina hottie in the storage room in the rear of the empty lingerie store. I squeezed her body against mine, ground my lips into hers, and thanked my lucky stars that had aligned in such a way as to keep Gillian away from work and put me on a collision course with the hot-blooded

Francesca.

She broke the vacuum seal on our mouths and I was left gasping. "Let's make some more room for ourselves," she said matter-of-factly. Drop-dead fuckable, and practical to boot. What a girl!

She reached past me and brushed aside the seduction-wear and the sales receipts that littered the counter and jumped aboard. She perched on the edge and held out her arms. I hastily and happily re-entered her airspace and felt her tongue lick my lips, then plunge into my open mouth. I met its wet-lightning heat with my own nipple-licker, and our tongues fought a ferocious battle that seemed to go on forever, ending in a win-win situation for everyone.

"Stick out your tongue," she said, her breath hot against my face, her body even hotter in my arms.

I stuck out my tongue.

She latched onto my slimy pleasure tool with her ruby lips and frantically sucked up and down its slippery length – like it was a cock just pulled dripping out of her steaming pussy. The heat and perfume from her body clogged my mental gears, and her passionate tongue-sucking snapped the tendons that held my body together and left me limp – in all but one important area. She might be young, but she sure as salsa knew what she was doing.

I gathered my strength and my hands sprang into action and found her tits. I began squeezing and kneading those luscious, shirt-splitting melons; gently at first, then more and more roughly. She liked it rough. I stuck my hands inside of her top and felt the hot, over-full nakedness of her brown bosom. She moaned into my mouth when I tweaked her engorged nipples, and her moan travelled down my spine like an electric shock and set my cock on fire.

"Suck my tits, big man!" she hissed into my open mouth. Her eyes blazed, her nostrils flared, and her chest heaved with uncontrolled lust. She was a girl who knew how to

136

handle her tits, and, in turn, demanded that they be handled. She shoved aside the thin cords that held her top aloft, exposing her overflowing treasure chest, and then placed her hands behind her, leaned back, and arched her back and offered up her big, bronze tits to the fiery sacrifice of my hungry mouth.

Had my mouth not been sucked dry, I would've drooled. Her breasts were even better out of the package – impossibly full and heavy, her nipples long and thick and chocolate-brown, her aureoles a good two inches in diameter. I swallowed hard and my throat clicked, and then I bent my head down and stuck out my tongue in prelude to licking her–

"What's going on here!?"

I almost swallowed my tongue in my haste to suck it back into my mouth. I jerked my tit-bound head to the left and there stood Gillian. She was staring angrily at us.

"Get back to the cash register, Francesca!" she ordered.

Francesca pushed me aside, refastened her top on the fly, and ran out of the storeroom, leaving me to face the wrath of Gillian alone.

"I don't think that our marketing agreement includes anything about you fondling my staff, does it Mr. Hull!?" she demanded.

My tongue was a slab of wood in my mouth.

She advanced into the room and said, "I always test out any new products before my staff does, anyway."

I stared at her, disbelieving, when she looked me square in the eye and began to slowly unbutton her stretched-to-the-max silvery, silk blouse. "I-I-I ..." I stammered.

"You've sampled one of my store's products, Mark," she said. "Now let's see what you think about a slightly different, older model."

I nodded dumbly as she finished with the buttons and pulled her blouse open and pushed it off her shoulders. It swished to the floor, forgotten. Her enormous tits were cupped by a black lace bra, similar to the ones I had brought to her earlier in the year. Her skin was ivory in contrast to the heavy-duty tit-holder, and her massive chest was heaving up and down with excitement. Her fingers shook as she unhooked her short, black skirt, wiggled her hips, and let the hanky-sized garment puddle at her feet. She was wearing a black thong over her nether regions. She lifted her stiletto heels out of the inert skirt and stood proudly in front of me like a statue of Venus come to life.

I gulped my admiration. Her body was a reflection of perfection – slim, smooth, and round in all the right places, and top-heavy with milky-white mammaries even larger than those of her well-endowed sales clerk. Her body shone in the light of the overhanging bulb, and her long, black, shimmering hair caressed her bare, buff shoulders.

"I've been waiting for months for you to make the first move," she said, her sky-blue eyes drilling into me. "But when you didn't, I thought that maybe you weren't interested, so I arranged for Francesca to get you interested. Are you still?"

The classic bait and switch sales technique. Like that much effort was needed in this erotic transaction. "I'm very, very interested," I gurgled.

Her blood-red lips tilted up into a smile, then parted slightly to allow her pink tongue to peek through. I boldly grabbed her in my arms and planted my lips over hers. She wrapped her arms around my neck and I felt her protruding nipples punch holes in my shirt. My shirt! Good God, this was no time for clothing.

I grasped her shoulders, pushed her back, and peeled off my shirt, shoes, pants, and shorts in the time it took a hummingbird to warble the first few bars of Stripper's Rhapsody. In that same short time, she also unsheathed her tits and pussy.

"You're beautiful," I gasped, staggered by her glorious, mature nakedness. Her tits were tremendous – huge and heavy and pink-nippled, and her pussy was blindingly bare except for a crown of soft, black fur.

"About time you noticed," she said. She jumped up on the counter where Francesca had proffered her window display only moments before, and assumed the same position and made the same heart-racing demand. "Suck my tits," she said huskily.

This time I wasn't going to stop even if my own boss barged into the storeroom with a Live at Five news crew; I was going to feed, dammit! I caught her tits in my hands and bent my head down and planted my mouth on hers. While my busy hands joyously explored her gigantic jugs, I kissed and tongued her relentlessly. I chewed her mouth like a starving dog chews a bone. I squeezed and fondled and groped her tits, caressing every inch of their incredible vastness.

I pulled away from her gasping mouth and went to work on her tits with my own mouth. I cupped their unbelievable heaviness in my hands and flicked my tongue against first one spectacular, inch-long nipple, and then the other. She moaned. I licked and licked her engorged nipples, bathing them in hot saliva, over and over, then nipped at them lightly with my teeth until they blossomed even further. Then I swallowed one in my mouth. I sucked and sucked on her left nipple, tugged on it, slapped my tongue across its inflamed, rubbery rigidity.

Gillian's body trembled. I attacked her right nipple – gave a repeat performance. "Oh, God, that feels good," she murmured, her eyes closed, her head thrown back, her bountiful breasts offered up for my taking.

I pushed her tits together and bounced my head back and forth between her fantastic globes, sucking on each nipple in turn, then desperately jamming them together and

139

sucking on both nipples at the same time.

"I'm gonna come, baby," she moaned, her arms quivering as she held her huge chest aloft for me to ravage. Her tits were obviously used to a lot of attention, and, as a result, very, very sensitive.

"Not yet, Gillian," I pleaded. "Not yet." Not before I had rammed my flaming cock into her fiery pussy and unloaded a megaton of come, or two.

We were obviously on the same sexual wavelength now, for she said, "Fuck me, then. Fuck my pussy!"

I reluctantly unhanded and unmouthed her tremendous tits, and then gripped her long, smooth legs and lifted them up until her slender ankles were resting comfortably on my shoulders. Her pussy lips were slick with love juice, the silky folds beckoning me to enter. I moved forward until my swollen, purple cock-head was knocking on her fleshy door of ecstasy.

I savagely pushed my raging cock forward and the glistening folds of her sopping womanhood parted and I slid inside. The heat and the tightness and the dampness were incredible. "Yeah," I hissed, as my cock found its home.

"Fuck me!" she screamed, pushing forward, burying me to the balls inside of her.

I began rocking my hips back and forth, sliding my steely shaft in and out of her; slowly at first, then faster and faster and faster – until my cock and my vision blurred. I pounded away at her pussy like she was my last fuck on earth.

"Yes!" she cried out, urging me to re-double my already frantic efforts. Her immense, saliva-slickened breasts bounced in rhythm to my desperate thrusting.

I tossed back my head and let out a roar as I banged away at Heaven's silky gate, my balls cracking sharply against her firm, round ass. Perspiration poured off my face, and I turned my head and kissed and licked and bit her

140

fleshy calf, in a reckless bid to hold the boiling semen in my sac for as long as I could.

"Come on my tits!" she yelled above the sweat-drenched frenzy.

That did it. My balls tightened and I knew that I was only seconds away from devastating detonation.

She beat me to it. Her eyes and mouth flew open and muscles tightened to the snapping point up and down the length of her sensuous body. "God, yes!" she screamed, and her upper body spasmed and her tits jerked up and down as she was wracked by orgasm. Her legs tightened on my neck, choking me, as she was brutalized, over and over, by powerful orgasms that laid waste to her body and mind.

She was no sooner torn apart by sexual ecstasy than I yelled, "Here I come, Gillian!" and pulled my flaming cock out of her red-hot lovebox and pointed it at her mammoth mounds and began flailing away for all I was worth.

"Come on my tits!" she cried again.

My hand was a blur, recklessly and relentlessly polishing my pole to the ignition point and beyond. "Yeah!" I screamed, then watched from a fluffy, floating cloud of pure ecstasy as frothy, white-hot come sprayed out of my cock and splashed down onto that gorgeous, experienced woman's tits.

"More!" she yelled. "Give me more!"

My body dissolved as I savagely stroked my cock and rocketed jism onto that big-breasted, come-hungry goddess. Thick ropes of super-heated semen erupted from my purple cock-head, again and again, and coated her tits and face in a white, gooey finish. I poured come down upon her like I had a never-ending supply, anxious, frantic to paint her beautiful breasts with my salty gunk.

I blew semen one final time, and then the tendons that held me together turned to jelly and I slumped against her legs, spent. I just about lost consciousness when Gillian leaned back flat on the counter and rubbed my simmering semen all over her hot, over-ripe body in long, sensuous, circular strokes, and then carefully and seductively licked her fingers clean of the sticky substance – one finger at a time.

She ran her tongue across her puffy lips and smiled a wicked smile. "Next time, maybe you can sample Francesca and me at the same time."

I nodded faintly. "I'll buy whatever you're selling," I groaned.

The New Physiotherapist
by Eva Hore

I have been seeing my physiotherapist, Ann, for years. The other day she broke her leg and now a locum is filling in for her. You should see him, he's absolutely gorgeous. Built like a body builder, extremely good looking and most importantly he's single. His name is Richard, but he goes by Dick.

I nearly died when I first saw him. I had no idea about what had happened to Ann and rocked up for my appointment wearing skimpy underwear. I nearly went home but then decided that was ridiculous, the guy was a professional, nearly a doctor and seeing me nearly naked, certainly didn't mean he'd attack me, well that's what I thought.

He asked me to strip off to my underwear and when I said how embarrassed I was, he just laughed it off.

'Look,' he said. 'In my line of work it means nothing. Whether you see Ann or me, it really doesn't matter. I'm like a gynaecologist, immune to being tempted.'

Okay, I thought. I peeled my baggy tracksuit off as he was reading through my notes. When he looked back up I'm not lying when I tell you that he actually gasped. I know I've got a hot-looking body. I used to be a stripper, highly paid, and so I'm used to guys drooling over me.

He actually blushed and I found it difficult not to laugh.

I thought I'd act dumb and innocent and as he set about putting me through some exercises. There was something there between us, chemistry or just plain lust. The more I stared at him, the more I decided I wanted him, wanted him right now.

He asked me to lie down on my stomach and I knew it would look to him as though I was naked. My g-string hugged the crack of my arse and my bra strap was whisper thin.

After applying heat he began to massage and manipulate my shoulders. He raised the height of the table and as he turned my neck I noticed I was only inches away from his crotch. Took all my will power not to grab his cock, which I might add was bulging in his trousers.

When his fingers went lower, into my lower back and he began to knead my arse cheeks on the pretence of getting into the sciatic area I thought I'd move things along a bit.

'Oh yeah, right there,' I said. 'A bit further over.'

He moved downwards, his fingers only inches away from the crack of my arse.

'Ann usually gets up onto the table so she can really put some pressure in there,' I said.

He hopped up, straddling me and when he touched a certain spot I pushed upwards complaining that it had hurt but when he tried to pull away I said it actually felt better and could he do it again and work up to my neck knowing he would be practically lying over me by the time he reached it.

His hands began to roam over me and I knew my perky arse would be far too much of a temptation for him.

'Oh yeah, that feels good,' I said. 'Hmm.'

His fingers ran down my spine and I felt the weight of him on the backs of my thighs. He was relaxing. He began to massage the cleft of my arse his fingers straying down the crack every now and again and I decided I needed to make my move.

'Ann also uses that sort of pressure on my groin area,' I said, quickly rolling over so he was now straddling my waist.

In the process of turning my breasts had popped over their cups. I pretended not to notice as I guided his hands into my groin. He was like a puppet. I manipulated him easily and when I thought the timing was right I cried out in pain and jack-knifed forward my hands shooting out to grab at him.

'You okay?' he asked, his face flushing, his eyes riveted to my breasts.

'Oh, yes,' I breathed against him. 'Sorry, it really hurt.'

My hands slid slowly down his chest, then over his belt buckle, straying just out of reach of his zipper and accidentally grazing his cock.

He looked directly into my eyes now and I saw his hunger reflecting back at me.

'Oh sorry,' I mumbled, my eyes not leaving his as my fingers began to tug at his zip.

He said nothing and within seconds his monster cock jumped out of his trousers. I snuggled down, inching my body between his open thighs, until I managed to take him into my mouth, my tongue gliding over his knob.

'Er, ah, no we shouldn't be....' His words trailed off as I sucked him deep in my mouth.

He pulled away from me and jumped from the table. I thought he was rejecting me and pouted, attempting to explain my behaviour. Instead, he made his way to the foot of the table, yanked my legs apart so my cheeks were balanced precariously on the edge and leaned in on the inside of my thighs.

His breathing was ragged, his eyes wild with longing. He licked his lips as I whimpered quietly, my tongue running across my top lip. Pulling the crutch aside he fell between my open thighs and nuzzled into my pussy. God, it was Heaven. Please, I lay back, caressing my own breasts, tweaking the nipples, eager for him to take me, yet loving what he was doing.

'Fuck me,' I begged.

He lifted his head, my juices all over his cheeks, chin and mouth. He tore at the flimsy material and ripped my g-string from me. I lay there, totally exposed and vulnerable, wanting nothing more than his magnificent cock to fill me up.

'Ohh,' I squealed, 'now I know why they call you Dick. What an amazing dick you've got there. I hope you know how to use it,' I challenged.

He didn't disappoint me. Leaning into my open thighs his knob probed my outer lips. I inched forward, eager to begin, my legs wrapping themselves around his back. He sunk his shaft in to the hilt. I've never felt a cock like it before. He slammed into me, fucking me like a man possessed.

Suddenly the phone rang. We looked at each other, wondering whether to stop. The intercom flicked on and the receptionist's voice reverberated around the room.

'Sorry to interrupt, Dick, but your wife is on the phone,' she said.

He stiffened, and by that I don't mean his cock. He looked apologetically at me before pulling away, my juices dribbling over his trousers as he lifted the receiver. Unperturbed, I scrambled from the table and knelt before him, picking up his slippery cock to lavish with my tongue. He was having difficulty speaking as my mouth slid up and down his shaft.

'I've got to go,' he said. 'I'm in the middle of something. I'll call you later.'

'You bitch,' he laughed, wiggling out of his trousers and kicking off his shoes.

I yanked at his shirt, popping most of the buttons, in my haste to see him naked. Within seconds he tore my bra from me and naked we grappled with each other before falling to the floor to take up where we left off.

With my legs wrapped around his back he fucked me so ferociously that I received carpet burns to my back and arse. I flipped him over and straddled his waist, impaling myself on his rock hard cock. Holding onto the desk I slammed into him as he grabbed at my breasts, pawing them with his fingers, tugging at the nipples, until I actually cried out.

He pulled me down towards his mouth and we kissed passionately as I humped him, slamming down hard, his knob hitting me where no other man ever has. My breasts were jiggling all over the place as I peaked, stiffening as my body spasmed with a much needed orgasm. As my juices flowed out of me and my body began to relax, he slapped me on the thigh and motioned for me to stand.

As soon as I scrambled to my feet he slammed me over the table, my perky arse titling up for him. I spread my legs, wiggling my cheeks, desperate for him to fuck my cunt some more, only he had different ideas. Prising open my cheeks, his enormous knob probed my puckered hole. With his fingers pulling me open, his slippery knob inched its way in.

I've never had a cock that big up my arse before and would never have believed he would fit but fit he did. Slamming in and out of me, he held onto my hips and shot some of his load deep inside before withdrawing and coming all over my back.

The intercom came on again. 'Your next patient is here.'

'I'll be right out,' he said, trying desperately to control the tremor in his voice.

'Here,' he said. 'Wipe yourself off.'

'You're not leaving me like this, are you?'

'Just for today,' he smirked, 'but I think I might have to

see you daily until this condition stabilises itself.'

'Really?' I said, sitting naked on the edge of the table.

'Yes. And if you feel the need, you can always give me a call on my mobile. I'm happy to do a home visit too.'

As he opened the door to leave, the secretary walked passed and looked in the partial open doorway. Her mouth dropped open as Dick walked on. Laughing to myself I ran my hands over my body, still feeling horny. Lying back on the table, I opened my legs and fingered my pussy. It felt so good, so I pulled the hood back over my clit and began to rub the nub, wanting another orgasm desperately.

I didn't have long to wait before my back arched and my body shook. With my eyes nearly closed and in the throes of coming I thought I heard the door squeak. I snuck a look over and sure enough there was an eye peeking at me.

The receptionist, no doubt.

I showed no reaction but did put on a bit more of a show for her. Then I set about getting dressed and quietly left the room. At the receptionist's desk I saw she was speaking briskly on the phone, her face flushed, her eyes shining with excitement.

As she made a date for me for the following day I leaned over the desk and whispered to her.

'Why don't you join us tomorrow?'

She eyed me before a smile played at the corner of her mouth. 'Make it 11.45,' she said. 'You'll be the last appointment before lunch, and tomorrow Dick is having a two-hour break.'

'Good,' I said. 'I hope to see more of you tomorrow.'

Laughing, I left the clinic, pleased that this new physiotherapist would be able to do more than just treat my body, he was treating me to many other things as well, and a threesome might just be what a doctor would order.

Mushroom Strudel
by AstridL

Simone left her Renault behind Steven's Jeep and ran to the
front door of the cottage. She pulled the fur-trim of her
hooded parka close about her cheeks, then she thumped the
brass horse-head knocker and waited. She thumped again.
Wiggling the round knob Simone found the door unlocked.
She pushed it open. A slapping sound came from the
kitchen. She edged closer.

A young woman in an oversized sweatshirt and large
woollen socks stood with her back to Simone. The girl was
engrossed in slapping a white mass onto a marble slab and
kneading it. Dark red curls tumbled over her shoulders. Her
hips rolled as she dipped to her knees, baring a decollete of
buttocks beneath French silk panties.

Simone cleared her throat. The girl spun around. Green
eyes looked Simone up and down. Simone felt a prickly
warmth creep up her neck. Who was this girl? Where was
Steven? What was she doing here in Steven's clothes?

"Bonjour," said Lucia.

"I was looking for Steven, the Englishman. Are you ... a
friend?"

"You could say that. My name's Lucia. You must be
Simone."

Simone froze. "How do you know? Where is he?"

Lucia turned back to the table, took up the white mass of

dough and slapped it once again onto the marble slab. "He went to chop wood," she said. "He was out all morning ... picking mushrooms."

Simone's eyes fell on the rough wicker basket heaped with autumn's spoils: yolk-yellow chanterelle; translucent grey oyster mushrooms; black, wizened morels; and the creamy-white king bolete with its brown, fleshy ridges on the underside.

"You have to be careful," she said. Lucia kept kneading. "I told Steven which ones were poisonous. There were some he didn't know."

There was something disturbing about the young woman. Simone felt her cheeks warm like a pre-heating oven, mixing emotions of jealousy, sadness and seduction like forest scents or fresh, yeasty dough. Simone slipped off her parka and hung it over the back of a chair.

"I'm making strudel," Lucia said. "Mushrooms. Wild ones. Although I shall mix in the shiitake." She turned her green eyes on Simone. "Don't you think they'd give it an exotic touch?"

Simone fingered the mushrooms in the basket. She glanced at Lucia bearing down on the dough. "Do you want me to help? Clean them?"

Lucia nodded. "Take that apron over there." She stopped, both hands resting on the dough. "The oven's heating. Don't you want to take off your pullover?" she said, her eyes travelling over Simone's ochre mohair.

Simone pulled off the mohair and attached the apron, slipping the fastened bib over her head. The apron skirt dipped down to protect her front.

"Perhaps knead the dough. It's quite tiring," Lucia said and sprinkled more flour on the counter. "So that it won't slip," she added and pushed a strand of hair from her forehead with the back of her hand causing tiny speckles of flour to trace her jawbone.

Simone wiped her hands on her apron and plunged both hands into the dough.

"Push down, Simone. Push with both heels of your hands. Draw the dough back with your fingers. Keep the rhythm."

Simone pulled and pushed, and pulled and pushed. Her whole body was moving in harmony. As she leant forward to push with the heels of her hands across the counter, her knees bent so slightly in a rolling motion that swelled through to her shoulders bearing down on the dough.

Lucia took a step back to gaze at the hypnotic movement. The only sound was the cool flap-flap against the marble and the sound of rhythmic breathing. Simone kept on kneading, eyes half closed.

"That's good," Lucia said and began cutting earth and rough edges from the mushrooms.

The pearly dough felt like silk in Simone's hands. She bore down, kneading, building up a gentle rhythm. It had a strangely calming effect, yet gave way to a prickling about her chest. As she loosened the buttons of her moss green silk blouse, her eyes met Lucia's.

The younger woman held the creamy crown of the king bolete and was plucking away the fleshy stem. She ran her fingers over the inside ridges almost as if in a caress. "It's so soft, so fragile," she murmured. "Yet so resistant."

Simone felt a triggering in her core and lowered her eyes to concentrate on the dough.

"Ever done this before?" Lucia asked.

Simone looked at Lucia. Her throat blocked the sound of her voice as she slowly shook her head.

"Mushroom strudel... I mean," Lucia said. Her green eyes laughed.

So she's calling my bluff, Simone thought. The strange thing was that it had become a game, and each layer of apprehension was slowly being stripped away. No longer jealous, Simone found she was becoming the object of Lucia's desire. It was an unusual and new feeling, even if it felt like being equated to the insides of a mushroom. Simone laughed.

Lucia looked up, puzzled. "May I share?" she asked.

"Seems to be what it's all about," she said. "The king bolete certainly is a magnificent specimen."

Lucia pulled off her sweatshirt and stretched her arms. "It's getting hot," she said.

"Indeed," Simone said with a smile.

Lucia looked down at her oversized socks and giggled. Her silk camisole top barely hid the tautness of her nipples. Simone felt a gentle wave push through her at the sight of Lucia's arousal. *How was this game to be played?* she thought. *Just let the wave carry you*, a voice inside her whispered.

Then Lucia came round to Simone's side of the table. "Aren't you hot? We're all alone here, you know. Just us girls." She smiled as she slipped the tape of the apron over Simone's neck and let the bib dip down to her knees. Simone closed her eyes as Lucia's fingers slipped each pearly button of her blouse through each snug buttonhole. Her breasts ached for attention as tiny ripples ran within her.

"You're lovely, Simone," Lucia whispered behind her ear and gently teased a finger about one nipple. It hardened instantly.

Simone's pulse raced. She didn't move, almost swaying in a trance to the stroking of Lucia's finger.

"There, that's better," Lucia said as she slipped the blouse from Simone's arms. Then she brought the bib back over Simone's head. "Want me to handle the dough a while?"

Simone nodded. She glided to the other side of the table. The mushrooms were soft and pliant under her fingers. She

152

cut through them easily with the sharp knife, like cutting through room-warm butter.

"I've already chopped the leeks, the shiitake and the walnuts," Lucia said. "Just mix them in and add the oregano, sesame seeds and pepper ... as you would in your own kitchen," she added with the hint of a smile.

Simone's fingers sifted through the browns and beiges and ambers, revelling in the change of textures from the soft and moist of the mushrooms and leeks to the hard, smooth feel of the walnuts. She added a generous dollop of soy sauce and mixed in some cooked rice, breathing in the precious aromas released by her ministrations.

Lucia rolled out the dough. "It has to be very thin," she said. "Almost see-through, like the silk of your blouse." One strap of her camisole had slipped from her shoulder. "We can spread the mushrooms. Come. Help me roll the strudel."

Simone carried the bowl of sliced mushrooms back to Lucia's side. A rich scent rose to her nostrils – an exciting blend of fresh dough, forest musk and a hint of jasmine. She could hold back no longer. She placed the bowl on the table and her lips caressed Lucia's shoulder. Gingerly she slipped a finger under the strap of the camisole bringing it back up Lucia's arm. Her hand brushed Lucia's nipples peaking through the sheer fabric. All she could hear was a faint swishing of silk and the beating of her own heart. With both hands Simone pushed up the camisole and buried her face in Lucia's breasts. Lucia sighed and caressed Simone's head. "It has to bake for 40 minutes," Lucia said. "Let's finish the strudel first."

Simone drew back, flushed. She watched Lucia expertly roll the mushrooms in the dough and place the horseshoe shape on a tray. With a brush she stroked melted butter over the top. "To make it glow," she said. Then she popped the strudel in the oven. Wiping her hands on Simone's apron, she said: "Do you trust me, Simone?"

They were breast to breast. Simone searched Lucia's face. "Yes," she said simply. This young woman had opened up new sensations, ones she had never known. She was introducing her to new delights, recapturing a youth she had let slip away. How could she not trust her? "Yes," she said. "I trust you, Lucia."

"Then turn around."

Simone turned, obeying as if in a trance.

From out of nowhere, Lucia slipped a black satin sash over Simone's eyes and tied a bow at the back of her head. Simone saw nothing, yet her senses were heightened. The scents of the forest, of rising yeast, of baking warmth, enveloped her. She heard the gentle dribbling of the tap in the sink, the swishing of movements. Lucia's? Was she leaving. Simone's heart raced again. She couldn't leave. Trust her. Trust her.

"I'm here, Simone," Lucia said. "Imagine. Just imagine a winter's warm dessert, the smell of nutmeg, cinnamon ..."

Simone closed her eyes beneath the sash. She could feel the warm tingle of cinnamon as a warmth rose around her. The back of a strong, gentle hand stroked her cheek. As firm fingers slipped down the side of her neck over her chest and large warm hands cupped her breasts, she smiled and stretched her hands out to feel lean, naked masculine hips beneath her palms.

Slowly she moved her palms to each other, her fingers outstretched, feeling the tight mound of an abdomen; the heels of her palms grazed coarse springy hairs and as her thumbs came together something strong, soft and alive nudged them away. Simone slid to her knees and took Steven's strength, knowing she must drown in the nutmeg taste of him.

154

Beach Baby
by Lynn Lake

I'm a lifeguard at Miami Beach, and the most amazing thing happened to me on my first day on the job.

I'd just gotten my high school diploma and Red Cross lifeguarding certificate, when I was hired by the Miami Beach Patrol and Ocean Rescue department. I was totally psyched, thinking about all the money I was going to make and fun I was going to have at the beach all summer long, before I started college in the fall. But I was still plenty nervous when I showed up at Ocean Rescue headquarters on Ocean Drive for my first day of lifeguarding.

I got there real early so I could go for a run and a swim with some of the other newbies. Then right at 7:30a.m., we all assembled inside to get our instructions.

"Ready to save some lives?" Lieutenant Don barked, pumping us up.

I didn't need any pumping. I was already so anxious I was almost peeing my one-piece, my nipples just about popping the thin material. But I yelled, "Yes, sir!" right along with everyone else.

Then I got my assignment: Tower #3 on South Beach, with Troy. He'd been a lifeguard forever, and I guess Lieutenant Don thought the guy could teach me a thing or two.

We snagged a ride out to the funky-coloured art deco

155

lifeguard tower in the jeep, then climbed up into it. Lifeguard on-duty hours are 9:00a.m. to 7:00p.m., but there were already tonnes of people on the beach. It was going to be one wicked hot day.

I checked our gear, and then Troy got me to raise the green flag, which meant 'calm conditions' on the water. I thought then maybe I was going to have a pretty easy first day, and I started feeling less scared.

"Why don't you do a walk-around, Lana," Troy said, "while I man the tower? Make sure everyone's following the rules and behaving themselves – the best way to deal with trouble is before it starts."

Troy's smart like that. So I scooped up my Rescue Can (an orange, oblong, plastic floatation device that we use to assist in rescues) and hit the beach. The sand was hot, but my feet soon got used to it. But I got nervous all over again; all those people in the water and on the beach – swimming, snorkelling, windsurfing, water skiing, sunbathing and playing games – looking to me for leadership.

I spotted some boys I knew from high school. They were tossing a football around, until they spotted me. Then they waved and started checking me out in my one-piece. I just nodded, totally all-business. But ... I couldn't help notice their shiny, brown bods and the bulges in their Speedos. In fact, I got so distracted I wandered right into this little girl's sandcastle.

I walked further down the beach, keeping a sharp lookout for beach rule violators and anyone having trouble in the water, making sure the windsurfers and jet skiers weren't going where they weren't supposed to. My body was all slick with sweat and suntan lotion, and my pussy was so damp I worried I was staining my swimsuit. I mean, there were guys – total hotties – everywhere, all golden and glistening and half-naked. And some of them were even coming up to me and hitting on me.

"Is your name Summer, 'cause you're hot?" this one older guy said, blocking my way.

He was super hot, too – big and built, with eyes you could swim in. I got so flustered I raised my arms to back him off a bit and accidentally whacked him right in the groin with my Rescue Can.

His friends thought that was really funny. And while they were all laughing, this blonde woman in a hot-pink thong (topless!) put her hand on my shoulder and said, "You've left me breathless – can I get some mouth-to-mouth?"

I just gaped at her big, naked, brown boobs, then blurted, "B-but you're not even wet!"

"Wanna bet?" she said, smiling and licking her lips.

Everyone laughed some more at that one, and I turned five shades of red under my tan. Luckily, Troy rescued me by blowing his whistle. He was up in the tower, pointing out at the water. There was a man splashing around out there, drowning!

I raced down the beach and dove into the water, not even thinking, just doing, my training kicking in big-time. I swam out to the man and grabbed onto him. He was actually only in about five feet of water – I could touch bottom – but he was having all kinds of trouble, going under and swallowing water and thrashing around and stuff.

I got him to grab onto the Rescue Can and then I started swimming for shore, little me towing this big guy along behind her. I guess my adrenaline totally kicked in, because I had no problem dragging him out of the water and up onto the beach. Then me and another guy rolled him over onto his back, and I kneeled down beside him in the sand. His eyes were closed and his lips were blue. He wasn't breathing. He was dying! But I knew what to do.

I tilted his head back and pinched his nose and locked my lips onto his, started blowing, giving him artificial

157

respiration like I'd been taught. He started spluttering, and I quickly straddled his stomach and started pumping his chest, trying to get him to cough up the water in his lungs.

There was a big crowd gathered around us by then, but even in the middle of all that excitement, I have to admit that I felt the guy's prick in between my legs. I couldn't help it – for some reason he was hard like a piece of driftwood, and huge. His cock pressed into my bum and against my pussy, as I worked his hairy chest.

Fortunately, after about the fourth chest-pump, the guy gushed water and the colour started coming back into his face. He was going to live! The crowd cheered, but I kept on pumping.

He spewed up more salt water. His eyes fluttered open. And then, he suddenly grabbed onto me – grabbed onto my boobs! He was all disoriented, I realise, didn't know what he was doing, but, man, he really latched onto my boobies. The crowd got all quiet. Then someone giggled, and they all started laughing. And so did I.

I didn't mind if the guy was handling my boobs, as long as he was going to be okay. But with him gripping my tits like that, it sure made me conscious of the fact I was sitting right on top of his hard-on.

Eventually, he coughed one last time and became coherent enough to realise what he was doing. He dropped his arms in the sand like my chest was electrified. Then Troy pushed his way through the crowd and helped me pick the guy up, get him back on his feet. Not before I kind of slid back and forth on his dong, though – just to feel what it felt like. It was naughty of me, I know, but it felt good, my pussy getting all tingly.

"Sorry about the …" the guy said, pointing at my boobs.

Troy stared at me, and I blushed. The people in the crowd laughed once more and then started walking away.

"My legs just cramped up on me," the man I'd rescued

said, "and I couldn't keep my head above water. Thanks a lot for pulling me out. You saved my life."

"All part of the job, sir," Troy responded. "Why don't you take him back to the medic station, Lana, so he can rest up a bit? Okay, sir?"

The guy nodded, and I put his arm around my shoulder and helped him up the beach, while Troy went back to the tower.

His name was Robert, and he was in his late-thirties or so, I guess, going kind of bald and a little podgy, but with a cute face. He thanked me ten times more before we got to the medic station.

Old Mr Jensen, the civilian desk clerk, was the only one around. He helped Robert fill out a form, the dirty old man staring at my boobs and butt the entire time. Then he watched me escort Robert into the patient room.

Robert grabbed onto the railing of the bed in the small room, still kind of shaky. I offered to get him a Gatorade or a chocolate bar or something – to help him get his strength back.

"No thank you," he said politely. "I'll be fine. I'm just a little dizzy, is all." He smiled at me. "I used to be a lifeguard myself, you know, but I'm a bit out-of-shape now."

"You're not out-of-shape!" I blurted, staring at the big boner still bulging the front of his swimsuit.

"Well, uh, thanks," he said.

I felt myself getting all hot and bothered again, so I quickly changed the subject. "Um, when were you a lifeguard?" I asked.

He told me he used to lifeguard in college – the same college I was going to in the fall. We chatted about lifeguarding and college, as I helped dry him off with a towel.

"Mind if I shake the sand out of my suit?" he asked.

"Oh, sure, no problem," I said, turning around.

I heard him pull down his trunks, shake them out. Then I just about jumped out of my skin when I felt a towel on my shoulders, Robert's hands on my shoulders.

"Let me dry you off," he breathed in my ear, rubbing me with the towel. "You've been so good to me."

I started trembling as he towelled me. Even though the guy was drying me off, I was actually getting wetter – where it counts.

He rubbed my bum and my legs. Then I felt something else rubbing against my bum – something not soft and fleecy; something hard and long. I spun around and almost fainted with surprise. Robert was totally naked, his big cock dangling between his legs and pointing straight at me!

I gulped. I mean, I'd seen a few boys' pricks – when they'd whipped them out without even asking – but never a man's cock before. Robert was humungous, pink and veiny, with a big, fat, shiny knob. I didn't know what to do. I stumbled back against the door, locked it. I didn't want old Mr. Jensen to come snooping around.

Robert smiled, his face beaming and his blue eyes sparkling. "Since you breathed life into me," he said, "I thought I'd return the favour."

I didn't have a clue what the guy was talking about. But he walked up to me and put his arms around me and kissed me. And I went all soft and gooey inside, my pussy going liquid. His lips were so soft and he was so gentle – not like the slobbering horndogs who usually kissed me. I threw my arms around him and kissed him right back.

I could hardly believe what was happening – me and a man old enough to be my father, who I'd just pulled out of the ocean on my first day guarding the beach, making out in the medic station, him totally nude and me just about. It was too wild to be true!

But things got a million times wilder when Robert pulled

160

his tongue out of my mouth and led me over to the bed, his prick bobbing along like a lifebuoy. He pushed me down onto the bed, and I sat there. Then he dropped to his knees in front of me. He pushed my legs apart and hooked his thick fingers into my one-piece and pulled the skimpy material aside, exposing my pussy.

He stared at my cooch, then up at me. I knew what he wanted to do now. I could hardly believe it. But I kind of nodded, all shaky and burny at once. He bent his head down and stuck out his tongue and licked my pussy.

"Ohmigod!" I yelped, my body jumping. I'd never had a boy do that to me before.

But Robert was a man, and he licked me again, and again, slowly, wet-stroking my slit from bumhole to clit. I just about melted. It felt soooo good. Way better than my fingers had ever felt.

I gripped the bed and gawked at Robert's bobbing, bald head, as he lapped and lapped my cooch. It was awesome! I shimmered all over. And I must've tasted pretty good, too, because he slurped me forever. Before pulling my pink lips back and tickling my puffed-up button with his tongue.

"Mmmm!" I moaned, totally blown away, primed to gush girl-juice straight into the guy's face.

He licked and sucked on my clit till I thought I would pass out. I bit my lip so hard it almost bled, clawing at the bed. Finally, he looked up at me, his lips and nose all shiny with my slime. "Have you ever gone all the way, Lana?" he asked.

I was too amped to even speak. I just shook my head real quick.

He stood up and pulled me off the bed. "Why don't you get on top of me like you did on the beach?" he suggested.

Then he lay down on the bed, on his back, his huge boner twitching against his stomach. My legs were so rubbery I could barely stand, so I sort of fell over on top of him.

I managed to climb up onto my knees over top his erection. And then I pulled my suit to one side like he'd done, exposing my cunt again. Robert grabbed up his prick and poked its fat head right into my pussy lips. I had no idea how he was going to fit even a little bit of it inside me, I'm so tiny down there.

He groaned as he rubbed my slit with his dickhead, probably surprised to find how wet and juicy I was. Then he grabbed onto my waist with one hand, holding his cock with the other, and started slowly lowering me down on his towering boner. His knob popped inside me, and we both moaned. I closed my eyes and bit my lip again, my legs quivering like crazy. But I sat further down on the guy's cock, Robert guiding me, impaling me.

It hurt just a little – at the start – but then it felt wonderful. I was straddling the guy just like I had on the beach, only this time his long, hard cock was stuck all the way inside my pussy. He started lifting me up and down and pumping his hips, his prick sliding back and forth in my cooch. I caught onto the rhythm, bouncing up and down on top of him.

"Fuck, yes!" he cried, his face all red.

I dug my fingernails into his hairy chest and really rode the guy, his prick almost splitting me in two. He grabbed onto my boobs just like before. Only this time he really groped them, squeezing and kneading and rolling my nipples. My whole body buzzed and my head got all dizzy.

We moved faster and faster, splashing together, his cock churning my tunnel. Then my pussy went into meltdown, and I flooded with heat – coming! I shook out-of-control with joy, experiencing my first-ever genuine man-inside-me orgasm. It was absolute bliss!

Robert gasped like a fish out of water, yanking his prick out of my burning cooch and spurting all over himself. I rode his big, furry balls, polishing his spasming shaft with my pussy lips and butt, the both of us squirting.

And the next day on the job, I wasn't nervous one least little bit. I was an experienced lifeguard now. An experienced woman.

Oz
by Beverly Langland

Dorothy had it right. There *is* no place like home.
Especially when you are smarting and I hurt plenty.
Usually, in time of trouble I ran for the comfortable safety
of Mother's arms. Even if that were possible she wouldn't
understand. Not now. Not after she had warned me that
something bad would happen. Of course it did, as bad
things tend to around me. Nothing global, but on the scale
of personal fiascos this one ranked higher than most. That's
saying something in a miserable existence dominated by
failure and disappointment. The evening started
innocuously enough, though it rapidly turned into a debacle.
As I said, I have a habit of doing the wrong thing, of
swimming against the tide. It's not intentional. I just never
seem to quite fit in. Maybe if I was pretty, or clever, or had
a great sense of humour. I'm not and I haven't.

So, what brought about this current calamity? After all,
choosing fancy dress for your first office party is hardly
taxing – for most anyway. Why then, out of the hundreds of
employees did I alone get it so wrong? Maybe I try too
hard, too keen to impress in order to gain acceptance? I
spent a tidy sum hiring a costume. After much dithering I
eventually chose my namesake Dorothy from the Wizard of
Oz. How apt, for I could not have been more out of place.
Only as I climbed the steps of the coach did I realise my

mistake. Too late, I discovered the party had a pirate theme. The other passengers eyed me curiously – smirked openly at the little girl in pigtails. To top it all my boss Barry sat on the coach with his girlfriend. She is pretty, slim – was appropriately dressed. In that moment I hated her more than ever. I know that sounds bitchy but what chance have I with girls like Sandi in the frame?

The only honourable course of action was to hide. Yet, one can hardly blend into the background – my usual modus operandi at social gatherings – dressed in blue and white gingham. Especially when surrounded by cutthroats and pirates. Talk about being cast adrift on the high seas! No one bothered to talk to me unless to make fun or utter some snide remark. No one except Danielle that is, and she had her own dark motive. I am not a fighter. I take perverse pleasure in licking my wounds. They remind me I am alive. I was so engrossed in my own misery that it took some time before I realised she had not come to mock – not yet anyway. I looked up when she touched my arm gently – was captured immediately by her pale, watery eyes. Of course, she was dressed as a buccaneer, but a more beautiful buccaneer one could not imagine. Danielle looked stunning.

"Dot, right?"

I nodded, braced myself against the slash of her tongue, though in truth I wanted to run and hide. Beauty intimidates me. The girls in the office had warned me about Danielle. She was older than the rest of us, remained aloof and therefore an enigma. Still, I expected the worst. Why should she be any different?

"Care to dance?"

What? I glanced at the dance-floor. Most of the girls were dancing in the same tight cliques they maintained at work – a barrier against outsiders like me. Was Danielle insane or simply trying to upstage everyone else and humiliate me? Out on the dance-floor I would be even more exposed.

I shook my head. "I don't."

"Nonsense! Those ruby slippers were made for dancing."

Danielle grabbed my hand, pulled me reluctantly onto the dance-floor. I was petrified! Everyone stared, including Barry and Sandi. I've always disliked people looking at me. Wallflowers stay shy of the glare of publicity. We tend to hover on the periphery, blend in to the shadows. Under no circumstances do we venture into the limelight – never! Danielle sensed my discomfort. "Ignore them." That was easy for her to say. She had legs that reached her armpits. Mine barely left the floor.

I shuffled them anyway, but I was too self-conscious to relax. Next to Danielle my movements appeared stiff and wooden. She danced with the self-assured confidence of a beautiful woman. Beside her I looked even more hideous than usual! I was confused why she had chosen me to dance with. Often girls befriend me to make themselves look good. Danielle had no need of such underhand tactics. I didn't know then that she had an ulterior motive. Office tattle had her marked as a lesbian. She must have heard the gossip, although malicious tongues didn't seem to bother her. If anything, she walked taller, an amused smile tugging at the corners of her mouth. I had dismissed the rumours as just that. Now though, I felt a little concerned. Why had she singled me from the crowd? It didn't help that as we danced Danielle studied me intently. I had to fight the feeling that she was hovering close like a graceful vulture. I grew suddenly anxious. I liked my new job, wanted desperately to make friends even though I already knew I didn't fit in. Association with Danielle could only exasperate the situation. I briefly caught her gaze and something in her eye made me uneasy. Recognition perhaps? All of a sudden I wanted to lose myself in the throbbing mass of dancers, to hide from prying eyes – to hide from Danielle.

Yet, there was no escape. It would be like running from a lone wolf towards the pack. Instead I lost myself in the music. Actually, it felt good to be out of the house, away from Mother and the constant tension that had existed between us ever since I had moved back home, tail between my legs. We had argued before I left. Mother didn't approve of parties, didn't approve of dancing, disdained life in general. The music played relentlessly, all the while Danielle watching me too closely, her penetrating stare making me ever more uncomfortable. I wished for the music to stop. At least then I could make some excuse, break free from the intensity of her gaze. Mother always says to be careful what you wish for. The dance music did stop then, only to be replaced by a slower ballad. The change in tempo was too abrupt for most and the dance-floor became strewn with self-conscious bodies trying to slink into the surrounding darkness. Danielle smiled. "Don't you hate it when they do that?"

I was too intent on escape to reply. I made to leave the dance-floor, to follow the herd. Danielle was too quick for me, again caught hold of my arm, stopped me in my tracks. She placed her hands on my hips, turned me towards her, continued to dance, swaying gently to the music, moving ever closer like a hunter after her prey. I was thrown off guard by her persistence, by her closeness, by her sweet perfume. By now most of the other girls had left the dance-floor or had been collared by one of the lads. For once, I fared no better. Danielle drew me into her web like an unsuspecting fly and once she had me she was reluctant to let go. So, I danced on, my only alternative an inelegant dash for safety. Thankfully the lighting had dimmed significantly, leaving the dance-floor in virtual darkness. Surely, no one would notice? No one would pay attention?

168

Still, I hardly dare look at Danielle as we danced together in slow rhythm. Instead, I found myself absently staring at the floor, downwards at long legs, at smoothly gyrating hips moving sensuously in time to the music. I looked up quickly when I realised I had become hypnotized by them – directly into those captivating blue eyes. If anything, they were brighter now. I could feel them boring deep into my soul. Danielle moved closer still, so close I felt her breasts pressing gently against my own larger bust. I swallowed nervously, my throat impossibly dry, although my palms were moist and tingling. Then, with calculated ease Danielle placed both her hands firmly on my bottom, claimed me as her own. Despite the deliberate and slow movement I jumped, my mind lagging by several seconds. "What's wrong? Never danced with a girl before?"

I didn't answer, couldn't answer. If only Danielle knew how desperate I was for physical contact – for contact of any kind. Maybe she did. Maybe my desperation was that obvious. It was certainly such that I didn't complain, didn't pull away, didn't care who watched. For a time I danced like a string-puppet, my arms limp and awkward at my sides. I shuffled my feet slowly but my mind raced, trying to catch up with events out of my control – uncertain what to do. Then, still in a state of indecision, I felt sure hands grasp mine, place them on Danielle's pert bottom in a mirror image of her own embrace. They shot to Danielle's waist as if her bottom were the burning fires of Hell. Actually, I had danced with other women before – at ballroom classes where there was often a shortage of male students. This felt completely different. Danielle stood too close, her contact too sure. She was embracing me, encouraging me to reciprocate.

Suddenly, her cheek was against mine, her pretty mouth close to my ear, "You're so sexy," she whispered. I danced on in stunned amazement. Had I heard her correctly? No one had ever proclaimed *me* sexy. I willed Danielle to whisper the words again, to shout them aloud for all to hear. It felt so good to be wanted. The dance-floor was still in relative darkness, muted shapes shuffling, gyrating all around, yet I felt as if a spotlight shone directly on Danielle and me, searching with its powerful eye, picking me out from the darkness, pointing its long finger – look, there she is! There's the fat lesbian.

I was broken from my reverie when I felt Danielle press her body sensuously against mine. I felt guilty then as if I had somehow stolen her affection. I had obviously sent out the wrong signals and would have to set Danielle straight. Later. After this one dance. She felt too warm to resist, so soft I could not let go. I pulled her closer, felt invigorated by my bravado – excited even – more excited than I had felt in a long time, more excited than I cared to admit. Danielle seemed to melt into my body, gently directed me with her hands, encouraging me to sway my hips in time with the music. She was playing me like a marionette and I followed willingly. Our eyes met often. I knew she wanted me, but did she know how she made me feel? For the first time in my life I felt desirable. Tonight of all nights! One dance, I reasoned. What harm could one dance do? The music played on and in my dream state what could only have been a matter of minutes seemed like blissful hours. I didn't want it to end. I was lost in time and space and when the music stopped, I was surprised by the depth of my disappointment.

"Dorothy?"

The question made me start and I realised with horror that the lights had gone up. Lost in the moment I had continued dancing with my eyes closed, soaking up the intimacy missing from my life. I felt confused and disorientated, unsure what to do next. It was as if I floundered in a sea of jumbled emotions, the turbulent waters dragging me ever deeper. I searched the horizon for my supposed workmates, for some lifeline of support. They looked on as bemused as I. No one came to my rescue, not even Barry. Then they were gone, had again closed ranks, and I realised in that instant that I no longer cared.

Danielle smiled, squeezed my hand and then headed towards the bar, her stride so confident it was almost a swagger. I followed in a daze, my legs weak and unsteady.

We settled at a small table in a secluded alcove away from the dance-floor and prying eyes. I sipped my drink nervously, enjoying the cool feeling as the iced liquid soothed my parched throat. The dancing had made me so hot. Or was it Danielle? I felt a bead of perspiration run down my throat and disappear between my cleavage, watched as Danielle follow it with her hungry eyes. "I'm not a lesbian!" I blurted rather louder than I intended. A group of young men standing close by fell silent and turned to stare at the plain girl in the curious outfit. They gave me their usual brutal appraisal before moving away, sniggering to themselves. I blushed, my cheeks glowing so hot I felt as if I were on fire.

Danielle found it impossible to suppress a chuckle. "I know," she answered matter-of-factly, "and strictly speaking I'm not either."

"It's just you... I thought..."

"I do fancy you. It's just that I generally prefer so-called straight girls. Most lesbians expect meaningful relationships, whereas I'm just in the market for some hot pussy." Danielle waited while my cheeks turned a brighter red. I was certain she was revelling in my embarrassment. I wasn't used to people being quite so frank about sex. None of my acquaintances talked so openly. "Anyway, I prefer to corrupt innocents such as you," Danielle continued softly, "it's deliciously debauched. You've probably guessed that I didn't approach you by chance. I've been watching you all

171

evening, ever since the outfit caught my attention."

"Oh..."

"Oz is one of my favourite films. I've always had a perverse fantasy about getting into Dorothy's knickers. Perhaps you understand now why I'm so looking forward to making you come on my fingers." She held out her hands in an act of supplication. "What can I say? Beneath this angelic exterior is a wicked witch trying to get out!" She smiled warmly and despite my unease, I couldn't help but smile also. "Beautiful smile," she whispered. She was definitely toying with me. This was some sort of mating game she liked to play.

"I'm engaged!" I lied lamely, as if merely uttering the words provided a magic barrier capable of diverting Danielle's unwanted attention. As soon as the words left my mouth, I realised how childish and naive I sounded.

"All the better. You're more likely to put up a spirited fight. I do love it when you girls wriggle so. It gets me hot – gets us both hot! I can already feel the heat spreading deep between my legs. If we're not careful I'm going to burn your tongue."

Outrageous! I couldn't believe such words could come out of Danielle's pretty mouth. Dirty language generally made me uncomfortable, yet this beautiful woman with the foul mouth intrigued me. I was certain her shock tactics were designed to be deliberately controversial. "Oh, don't worry Dot, I'm not going to eat you – not yet anyway! But I am going to get into your knickers, if not tonight, then soon."

"Never!" I said with more confidence than I felt.

"Good girl! That's the spirit. But are you so certain? I have an intuition about these things. Intuition borne from experience. I've met many lonely girls like you. Outwardly defiant and proud. Ultimately weak and willing."

"I'm not –"

172

"– a lesbian. You've made that quite clear. No, Dot, you are something far more special. You're a submissive little tart. I on the other hand am a domineering witch. We two are opposites drawn towards each other. Can you feel it? It's a powerful, intoxicating attraction. I'm going to make you my love bitch!" Danielle paused, searched my face for some reaction, but I was too stunned to say or do anything. "I can ease your sense of alienation, Dot. Search your heart; you know it to be true. Beneath your false bravado is a little girl just pining for a good spanking."

"Spanking? Now wait –"

"Of course, you'll deny your feelings for some time, but deep down you already know the truth." I shook my head, turned away. "Look at me, Dot. Look at me!" I looked into the piercing blue eyes of my tormentor and I knew that Danielle could see the truth. I desperately wanted to prove her wrong. She knew I was weak; somehow sensed I was looking for someone stronger to guide me, knew that I needed a firm hand. It was too late to deny it, that one pathetic look told her all she needed to know. She was a hunter after all, a bully like all the rest. There was no point fighting now – she knew. She knew!

I looked up and caught Danielle smiling to herself. "I have my claws in you, Dot, it is inevitable now that you will give yourself to me. I excite you. Why do you think that is? The idea of me forcing you to do something wicked against your better judgement?" Danielle edged around the table, leaned in close, whispering into my ear. "Is there a dirty girl hiding behind that innocent facade? Does she want to come out and play with Danielle? I bet you're wet right now just thinking about it. Are you wet, Dot? Nasty, wicked Danielle is going to force her way into your knickers and the idea is making you wet with anticipation!"

"Stop it. Stop it!"

"Come now, I've been through this charade before. You

pretend you are horrified, but inwardly you want me to take you, want me to use you, want me to lead you down the path of temptation."

I felt sick to my stomach. The horror was Danielle was right. I wanted this. The verbal taunts were part and parcel of the seduction. An essential part of the foreplay. It raised the level of anticipation until the tension was at breaking point. Hers was a dangerous game. I knew Danielle would lead me out onto the parapet, would push and push until there was nowhere else to go except over the edge. Yet, only I could jump.

"I thought you liked me?"

"I do, Dot, I do! That's why I don't want you to be ashamed of who you are."

I was unable to decide what to do. I stared intently at the melting ice cubes in my glass, slowly jiggling them like tealeaves, trying to divine their meaning. There was no reason to stay, every reason to leave. I felt out of my depth, felt like a naughty schoolgirl caught somewhere I knew I shouldn't be. I looked directly into Danielle's eyes, searching for reassurance. "I'm frightened."

"That's okay, Dot. I understand. Truly, I do."

I found sanctuary in the Ladies' cloakroom, thankful for once that it was busy. All of the cubicles were engaged, so I headed for the sink at the far end of the room, turned on the tap, splashed cold water onto my face. I felt so hot! I had never met anyone as outrageous as Danielle, and although her words were appalling I was more shaken that I found her direct manner arousing. I admit I was flattered. For anyone to find me attractive – man or woman – felt agreeable, especially so when my admirer was someone as beautiful as Danielle. All the same, no good could come of it and besides, surely Danielle was only toying with me? It was time to end the titillation. I looked at myself in the

174

mirror. The bright-eyed girl who stared back was not as plain as I remembered, not as fat. Still, why would Danielle want me? There were conventions to follow, rules to obey. Wallflowers went home alone. We fell asleep crying or made love to our hand. Only rarely were we rescued.

I fished in my handbag for my make-up, paying little attention to the bustle taking place around me. Then I stood adjusting my hair, reapplying lipstick that didn't need improving. I didn't usually bother, so knew it was merely a delaying tactic, an excuse not to return to Danielle. I needed time to think! My mind was still a whirl of confused emotions. Danielle seemed intent to have me whatever I said or did. Thinking about that only made me tremble. I was disgusted, intrigued, frightened, and excited all at once. My hand shook so badly I had to give up trying to apply eyeliner. I took a deep breath, tried to calm the butterflies constantly in flight inside my stomach, held onto the edge of the sink for support, adrenaline pumping through my body. I felt exhilarated. To think! Someone wanted me badly enough they were prepared to just take me.

I hurriedly packed away my make-up, ran more water into the sink, bending once more to splash cold water onto my face, enjoying the cooling freshness against my heated flesh. When I raised my head, Danielle was standing beside me. I don't know why her presence was so unexpected. All the same, she made me start. She smiled at me wolfishly, the hunger in her eyes abundantly clear. I let out a pathetic whimper, certain she intended to devour me there and then. The path to the exit lay clear, yet I felt trapped. I looked about nervously. Several of the cubicles were still engaged, though I felt certain now that no one could save me.

I watched helplessly – like a rabbit caught in the full glare of a car's headlights – while Danielle placed her hands on my hips and drew me close. She kissed the nape of my neck and if such a thing were possible in the twenty-first century, I swooned. I felt as if my heart had stopped, as if all the air had deserted my lungs. My legs gave suddenly and I had to lean into Danielle to stop myself from falling. Then, still in my dream-state, I watched as she reached around me and placed her hand on my breast. Danielle observed my reaction in the mirror, her eyes glued to mine. I stood transfixed as she undid the bib of my dress, fingered and played with the buttons at the opening of my blouse. "Do you like watching?" she whispered against my ear.

I couldn't answer. I had no will of my own, had no control over my body. I had lost the facility to speak, lost the will to move, to struggle, to resist. Instead, I stared at my reflection as Danielle slowly undid one and then a second button of my blouse. She tugged the folds apart, laid waste to my bra, the material showing no more resistance than I. I wanted to shout out. I wanted to scream. I didn't. I couldn't. The best I could manage was a slow, breathless moan as she reached inside and cupped my naked breast, catching my nipple deftly between her fingertips. The nipple stiffened and grew at her touch. Danielle's hand felt so cool, so soothing against my burning flesh that I could find no reason to complain. Then her other hand joined the first, cupped and squeezed my other breast. This time my moan was louder, less guarded. I continued to watch with narcissistic fascination as Danielle's nimble fingers undid the third and final button of my blouse and set my porcelain-white breasts free. And like a porcelain doll I still hadn't moved, still hadn't raised any objection. I couldn't believe I was allowing Danielle to undress me in public. The whole situation became surreal – became my worst nightmare, my best fantasy. Danielle continued to knead both breasts with practised hands while I watched, fascinated as her red-tipped fingers worked their magic. I became a stranger in my own body. Surely, these breasts weren't mine, these alien feelings surging through my loins did not belong to me.

A young woman entered the cloakroom and headed for the first cubicle, seemingly not noticing Danielle and her finger-puppet at the other end of the room. The sound of her stiletto heels on the tiled floor awoke me from my hypnosis. I had forgotten where we were. When I realised, fear filled me and I struggled for the first time. Danielle seemed unperturbed, held me tight, content to continue with her seduction. She kissed my neck again took both nipples between thumb and forefinger, rolled them, tugged them – deliberately hard, I felt. I bit my bottom lip. I wanted my torment to end. I didn't want it to end. Oh God, it was inevitable that someone would catch us. I was a nice girl, a good girl. Mother often warned me of the evils of the world. Yet she never prepared me for this! I quickly scanned the room, spotted the CCTV camera, groaned inwardly as its red light winked at me knowingly. Part of me didn't care. Part of me wanted to be caught, wanted to rebel. Most of all, I didn't want my suffering to stop!

I turned back to the mirror, my focus back on the slender red-tipped fingers tugging at my nipples, on the fierce blue of Danielle's eyes. It was hard to believe I let this woman – a virtual stranger – use my body in this way. Suddenly, a noise caught my attention. I watched in horror as the door of the cubicle directly behind opened and a slim, redheaded girl stepped out. Sandi of all people! Danielle smiled as if she had been waiting for this moment, as if everything that had passed between us had led to this. As Sandi approached Danielle released me, exposing my breasts to the girl now standing at the sink beside us. Sandi's mouth fell open in surprise, and then before she could recover, Danielle reached up and once more took hold of my enraged nipples, squeezing them, stretching them. I wanted the ground to open and swallow me. The shame. The humiliation. Lord, the exquisite pleasure!

I felt liberated, alive for the first time. I forced myself to look directly at Barry's stunned girlfriend, challenging her to comment – to judge. For a moment our eyes locked and all I could focus on were her dark pupils, wide and accusing. For some reason her reproachful glare stoked the fire burning between my legs. I needed Sandi to say something – anything to affirm that this was real, to let me know I wasn't dreaming. She remained silent, her wide mouth slightly agape, but her accusing eyes spoke volumes. I know she blamed me. I was the tart with my tits out. I was the dirty slut. Danielle's bitch!

Suddenly, Danielle broke our silent battle of wills, turned me towards Sandi. "Want a feel, love?" It was too much, the humiliation too great. I felt my pussy implode, the shock waves radiating down my thighs, up across my abdomen. My stomach tightened. I clenched the edge of the sink, needing to hold on to what little reality remained. Through blurred vision, I caught sight of my contorted face in the mirror. I didn't recognise the girl staring back, face flushed, eyes glazed. It wasn't an orgasm of earth-shattering proportions, even for me. Yet, it was frighteningly real, horrifically obvious to us all. Sandi hurried from the room blushing, muttering moral indignation all the while. Tears welled to my eyes as I watched her leave. I felt ashamed, sick to my stomach.

Danielle still had hold of me. "Please…" Even I wasn't certain if I was begging for more of the same or pleading for Danielle to release her hold over me. Our eyes met in the reflection of the mirror. "Don't let me fall," I pleaded.

"I won't, baby, I won't."

Another cubicle door opened. Danielle released my breasts, patted my bottom affectionately. "Come on, Dorothy, let's get out of here!" So saying, she marched smartly out of the powder room, leaving me transfixed to the image in the mirror – an image of a dishevelled, innocent girl – lost and far from home.

I knew all I had to do was click my heels three times and I could escape. It was already too late. I had fallen for the wicked witch, had discovered something I was good at, had found somewhere I belonged. I didn't want to go home. Not yet. Not yet! Perhaps Dorothy got it wrong after all. All I know is that sometimes there is no happy ending. Sometimes – just sometimes – there's no place like Oz.

Italian Island Liaison
by Mark Farley

"You smell of sex..." my husband challenged me. He guided me into my seat in the restaurant and kissed the top of my head, which I suspect is how he sensed the presence of the 19-year-old I had fucked on the beach, a few hours earlier.

"That would be because I had sex, darling." I offered. I pondered over the entrées on the menu.

"Enjoy?" he countered, flicking through the wine list.

"Very much..." I inform him. "The sea bass sounds delicious."

We have been married for twenty years. We were at college together. No kids to speak of, we both had our careers in the city. The usual story, not that either of us have ever taken exception to it. In fact, we love the freedom to be able to jump on a plane and go and see foreign lands.

The reason why he wasn't either screaming at me and making a scene or walking off like most rational partners would do at this sort of admission is because we had come to a mutual agreement some time ago.

The sex had died down after the first ten years, we became more like flatmates in one room and we came to an understanding that we were both attracted to others. The turning point was when I found some illicit texts on his phone illuminating certain attributes down below and alluding to certain desires my husband has, from someone called Tia.

When he expected the slap around the face I hit him with something better.

"Okay then, you wanna play it like that... I'll fuck who I want to, then."

He laughed nervously and called my bluff. Two nights later, I went to Paper with some friends from work and brought a guy home with me.

"Oh, this is my husband..." I introduced the rather surprised 25-year-old Foxton's agent with a flick of my wrist. Well, I was wearing my wedding ring. Where did he think I was taking him when I grabbed him by the crotch on the dance-floor and whispered up into his ear that I was dying to take him home? If he doesn't do the ring check like 90 per cent of other guys do, that's not my fault, is it?

To my husband's credit, the first thing he did was offer him a beer and point him towards the Durex, to the utter bemusement of the tanned (if slightly portly) notch on my about-to-be-liberated bedpost. I took him into our marital bed and let him screw me rather vigorously, much to what I am sure was a little secret envy and frustration from downstairs.

Otherwise I hadn't really cashed in the open relationship card since I caught him, and that was two years ago, so I think my actions on the beach were entirely justified that evening, especially as he has two girls on the go back home who he sees most weeks. When I heard he'd had his first threesome with one of them and her husband, I figured that it was high time to start cashing cheques and have some fun myself.

I could have easily joined them.

In fact, he asked me. Twice.

They wanted a swap with us but I explained that I was

182

ready to sow my wild oats a little further, and it was something I was intending to do entirely on my own. Plus, the whole idea of wife-swapping seemed so passé, something people did in the Seventies, not to mention the threat of disease and the rest of it.

Our summer holiday this year gave me the perfect opportunity to catch him completely unawares. When he told me that we were going to Sardinia, I made a special effort to search out the nudist beaches and, after one false start when we stripped off and a young German family camped out next to us fully-clothed, we sauntered away in full naked glory and found our spot to make love under the hot Mediterranean sun.

This was in full view of a group of people, something he had always wanted to do, he happily said as he grunted away in my ear and pounded my splayed torso with his hips. It was after a heady day of sunbathing and we were both glad of the release. A nude swim and further shagging followed in the clear, shingled waters.

On the day of my misdemeanour, though, we had a wonderful lunch and attempted to get a tan. After a while, he was itching to get back to the hotel and book a tour to a nearby historical walled city for the following day. I told him that I was nicely settled and had every intention of getting through some more of the latest issue of *Vanity Fair,* specifically the interview with Angelina Jolie, that I had been enjoying.

"I'll be fine here. I'll meet you back in the room in a couple of hours."

He collected himself and made the mutterings of someone who was going to miss an opportunity if he didn't go. I both humoured and nurtured his idea, until he felt satisfied leaving me. In fact, I had to insist.

"I'll follow you up soon, don't worry."

I had absolutely no intention of doing that at all. There

was no way that I was just going to lay around in the nude with all this opportunity on offer. Actually, there was a rather suspicious look on his face when he realised that he was about to wander away from his naked wife and that I perhaps had intentions of my own. What he didn't know was that I was definitely going out to find some young stud and have him take me over one of the rocks.

As soon as he was out of sight and heading up the sand back towards the hotel, I put the marker back in my novel and organised myself straight away. I rubbed coconut lotion on my shoulders and the globes of my chest and tied my sarong around my exposed, bottom half. I put my book in my holdall and draped the towel over it. With that, I went in search of sex.

More than anything, actually, I thought it would be a nice chance to explore alone. To collect my thoughts and have a nice topless stroll, something I hadn't done by myself for a long time. Earlier, I had noticed a nice little cove divided from the main stretch of the beach by some secluded rocks, so I decided to take a walk over to see what I could find.

I found more secluded spots, quiet hidden nooks, and by means of climbing a little, one where a young man lay in his Speedos. He had a smooth, taut body and curly brown hair and looked a little like a young Charles Dance.

Instantly, I felt a pang inside me. I had found my suitor.

As I stepped down from the rocks and onto the sand near where he was sunbathing, I caught him looking up at me and admiring my exposed boobs. I noticed that the book he was reading was in French, so I struck up a conversation.

"Bonjour, Monsieur. Ça va bien ici?"

"Oui, merci..." he replied.

I continued in French (and will spare you the translation) much to his surprise. He could clearly tell by my boldness, lack of tan and accent that I wasn't French.

A good education in a top school in Montreal has suddenly paid off, I thought.

He seemed quite happy to continue talking to me in his native tongue. We momentarily ran short of conversation (my ignorance, I'm sure), so I turned towards the sea and walked to the water's edge. I kicked the water playfully and waded in up to my ankles.

I stretched and looked back up the shore where I had come from. I untied the sarong and stuffed it into my bag, turning round to ensure the young guy got a good eyeful of what was on offer. I took a look back towards him from behind my shades and noticed a nice growth in his Speedos.

I waded out of the water and back onto the sand. I stopped beside him, about twenty feet away and threw down my towel. I sat upon it and dried my toes with one of the corners. I brushed off the droplets of water and excess sand and, out of the corner of my eye, saw him slip a hand into his pants to adjust himself. I asked him very cheekily if it wouldn't be easier if he just took them off.

"Il serait plus facile si vous les enlevez?"

"Je pourrais faire, si vous n'avez pas d'objection?"

He said he would if I didn't mind.

"Come on," I thought. "Why are you shy, I'm already naked here."

I got to my feet and skipped over the gap between the towels and knelt next to him. Oh Jesus, let me just offer to do it myself and kick the elephant off the beach and get on with it.

"Peux-je les prendre pour vous?"

He grinned and went crimson. I looked around to spare his blushes a little and peeled his Speedos down over his bum to reveal a waxed, tanned groin. It certainly looked as if he wasn't averse to some naked sun-worshipping himself, so I guessed he was just being modest with me.

I ran my index finger up his length and tickled his balls.

I didn't want to dive straight in so I lay to his side. He rubbed one of my breasts and tweaked my nipples, which I just love. I urged him to tweak them harder. He obliged and I let out a little moan. The fresh sea air and growing desire were doing wonders for my sinuses and already I could sense a crescendo building up inside me. I grabbed his shaft with both hands and immediately sank my mouth down as he gasped something I shouldn't translate.

Sitting on his elbows and leaning back on the towel, I pushed him back flat with my hand and brought my rear end round to straddle his face. He tasted lovely and I've never sucked a man off with so little hair. I made full use of this and licked around the whole area, which I was used to being covered in thick curls. He was sea-fresh from a swim and his balls were musky with a hint of some sort of deodorant. I actually found it quite pleasant, licking the shaft and his groin. I licked further between his legs and around his arsehole, just like my husband likes. He grunted with his tongue in my hole and I heard him laugh.

He certainly knew his way around a pussy with his mouth. He nibbled and sucked on my labia and darted his tongue in and out like a seasoned veteran and soon had me bucking wildly. He even played with my arsehole!

Honestly girls, he hadn't even told me his name. The cheek of it!

I wasn't complaining though. He pushed back the soft brown hair getting in his way and pushed his tongue into my hole. His ferocity at times showed a lack of timing, but I was quite happy regardless. Especially pumping his erection in my fist and pushing him down with the palm of my hand on his chest.

I didn't want to give this boy a heart attack or overwhelm him with excitement so I quickly got off, reached in my purse and tore a condom from its wrapper. I popped it into my mouth and went down on him, slipping it

186

on with my teeth.

The sun was going down and turning a lovely orange colour and dipping behind the rocks as I pulled up my friend by the hand and led him over to the ridge and a collection of rocks.

I wondered whether I should ask his name at this point. Surely, it was far too salacious of me to have him take me without knowing who he was. Fuck it, I thought. This is my moment of sin. My hour of liberated fun. I don't need to know.

I bent over one of the rocks at waist height. I was offering it to him and he started to fumble and play with his cock. The condom had killed him. I turned around and dropped to my knees, getting him hard once again.

Take two, and he was away; he eased in and grabbed the extra flesh on my hips and ground away nicely. He kept going for a good fifteen minutes until I moved back and prompted him towards the towel. He placed me on my back and climbed on top.

We momentarily stopped and he pulled a towel over us as we heard the rustling of footsteps above us. I sensed that he was attempting to protect my modesty. I urged him to carry on. I wasn't concerned who saw us at this point and neither I guessed was he, kneeling on his calves and taking a heel in each hand, exposing my front to those who might be having a little peek.

When we had finished he tossed the soiled rubber behind him, looking like the cat that had got the cream, and I tutted at him. He got up obediently and retrieved it. He crumpled the soiled, sandy material in his fist and rolled back to me. We looked up at the trees and sensed the movement of people nearby.

I actually really felt like staying and having a hug but I didn't want to send out the wrong signals, so I collected my things and put my shades on.

I said goodbye and headed back up the beach, leaving my conquest satisfied and curled up with his book on the sand we had warmed. No doubt hoping that someone else would soon join him.

Hitch-hiking
by Izzy French

It was late. I was cold. I needed to get home. I held out my thumb. Were people more reluctant to stop for hitchhikers these days? I shivered, stepping into the road when the pavement ended. And the shiver was for more than just the cold. I was taking a risk, wasn't I?

Expecting a complete stranger to pick me up and take me towards home. Cars flew past, the drivers staring straight ahead. Pretending they couldn't see me, no doubt, not wishing to inconvenience themselves. I was a stranger to them, too, I could be anyone, after all. They might think I posed a danger. I kept walking, comforted by the fact that Jake would be waiting for me at home. He'd be cross I was late, annoyed I let the battery on my mobile die. We would row and make up by having sex, angry, urgent sex. The best kind in my opinion. Just thinking of it made me horny. And, anticipating sex tonight, I'd prepared a couple of surprises for Jake that would bring a smile to his face. I was beginning to enjoy my daydream.

"Hey, can I give you a lift?" I jumped. I hadn't heard the car draw up. I leant down and peered in to see a man's face. He was hard to make out in the dark.

I hesitated, but just for a moment. I'd stuck my thumb out, after all, what else had I expected to happen? Though I did feel a frisson of something – excitement, trepidation, fear, maybe?

"Could you drop me off in town? I could walk from there, it's only five minutes." I was taking a huge risk. But it'd be something to include in my sex talk with Jake later. If I dared. I opened the passenger door and stepped in. The seats were leather, the dashboard looked like real wood, walnut I thought. Impressive. I knew nothing about cars, but guessed this guy had money. I glanced over. I could see him more clearly now we were closer together. His hair was dark, wavy, longish, his lips full. I thought his eyes were blue, but it was impossible to tell for sure. He wore a cream shirt, dark blue jeans, both looked casual but I thought the effect was contrived. This man was immaculate. His aftershave was expensive, delicious. I wondered if a beautifully groomed girlfriend had bought it for him. I looked down at my own clothes. An old leather jacket of Jake's, a light cotton top and a knee-length denim skirt that had risen up my thighs as I sat down. Only my high suede boots kept my legs warm. I wondered what he thought of me. I must look under-dressed for the weather. Perhaps he took me for a prostitute rather than the more prosaic office manager that I was.

"Warm enough?" His voice was icy cool and deep. A confident man, I thought. I nodded. Soft jazz played on the stereo. I relaxed back into the seat. I could feel warm air circulate through the car. It had been a long day and I was tired. I closed my eyes, feeling myself drift towards sleep. I began to dream. Jake and I were kissing. His hands stroked my face. Then I woke with a start. It wasn't Jake's hands. It was his, the driver's. I didn't know his name. His fingers were tracing over my right cheek, down my neck, resting on my top. I looked round.

"Sorry," he said, not sounding it. "Your skin's beautiful. I had to touch you." Not the kind of man who asked permission.

I stared at him. Eventually he pulled his hand away. There was silence for a few minutes as we drove. Then he pulled off the main road onto a rural lane. This wasn't the right way. I knew that of course, but I said nothing. My stomach was full of tiny butterflies. I squirmed in my seat. But still I remained silent. He spoke first.

"Okay if I pull over?"

I nodded my assent. We glanced at each other. His gaze was appraising, his eyes roved over me. I felt naked and crossed my arms across my chest. I could hear my own breathing, shallow, quick, excited. Stop soon, I thought. I can't bear the waiting. As if he'd heard me he pulled the car into a gap by a farm gate and switched off the engine. Without the powerful purr the silence felt tangible, like a wall between us. Until he reached over.

"Take off your jacket," he commanded, touching my shoulder. And I did, throwing it onto the back seat. His fingers were warm, his touch light. This time they traced down to the top of my arm, pulling my top away. He leant over and just barely kissed my exposed flesh, his lips skimming over my arm and shoulder, his tongue wetting my skin, his hot breath following on. My eyes were closed.

"Turn to me," he said. And I did. His hands cupped my face now and then I felt his lips on mine, insinuating a kiss from me, forcing my mouth open, his tongue pushing its way in, entwining with mine. Desire flooded through me. I responded, exploring his mouth in turn, pressing my lips against his, biting gently with my teeth, him reciprocating until my lips began to feel bruised, sore, but alive with tingling need. I shivered. My top was thin, fine cotton and a snug fit. It was one of Jake's favourites. I wore no bra, one of the surprises I had ready for Jake. My nipples were erect, pressing against the fabric, clearly visible. He looked down at them.

"I want your top off. Now. Over your head."

"It's too tight," I replied. "There are buttons at the back."

"I can't fuck around with buttons." The words sounded strange uttered in his cultured, cool tone. He reached round my back and pulled my top apart, buttons flew all over his car. He discarded the slip of fabric somewhere near my jacket. My breasts were exposed now.

"Raise your arms." I did what I was told. My breasts felt full, heavy with lust, needing to be touched.

"Shame about your top," he said. "It was pretty, but these are prettier." His hands cupped my breasts, his fingers squeezing pleasure from my nipples. My body felt aflame now. There was no danger of the cold outside having any effect. I threw my head back, his lips grazed my nipples, licking softly at first, then biting, chewing, sucking. The wetness on my breasts, from his saliva, was echoed in my pussy. I squeezed my legs together, already feeling close to orgasm. Having my breasts caressed like this had that effect.

"Over here. Come on." With the push of a button his seat flew back and then reclined. The action was smooth. He helped me over the gear stick and handbrake, my breasts bouncing close to his face, and I straddled his legs, the suede of my boots brushing against the expensive denim of his jeans.

"Knickers go next I think," he said as he pushed his hands up my thighs and under my skirt. There was Jake's second surprise. I wasn't wearing any.

"Fuck me, did I pick the right hitchhiker tonight." He pushed my skirt up round my waist and cupped the cheeks of my arse, pulling me down his lap. Much as I was enjoying this, and I certainly was, the moist spot left on his jeans by my juices told us both that, I felt at a slight disadvantage. I was almost naked, he was still fully dressed. He had been in charge so far; it was time for me to take control and for him to see what I was made of. I placed my hands either side of his open-necked shirt and tugged. His buttons fell into his lap and he brushed them away.

"I like a woman with spirit," he whispered as I ran my hands over his smooth, muscular chest, tearing his shirt from him and added it to the pile of discarded clothes. Though it was dark I could clearly see the bulge of his erection pushing against his jeans. That could wait, I thought. There was more I wanted him to do to me first. And at that moment I could tell he was feeling the same. With one hand he raised me slightly from his lap, whilst he pulled the other forwards down the crack of my arse and thrust his fingers deep into my dripping cunt.

"Fuck me," I cried, surprised at the suddenness of his movement.

"I intend to," he replied. "But not just yet." I opened my legs and rocked backwards slightly, allowing him as much access as possible. My pussy clenched around his pumping fingers and I could feel cool air around my clit. He allowed me to fall to his lap and twisted the fingers of his other hand into the curls of my mound, searching for my clit, which was begging for his attention. Parting my lips he caressed and rubbed until I felt my orgasm almost overwhelm me, my pussy tightening around his fingers. He'd done this before. He was good. I drew back from him, pulling his fingers out of me. I wasn't ready just yet.

He looked up at me, as if to say, what now? But remained silent. With little room to manoeuvre I got onto my knees, placing my pussy at the same height as his face.

"Lick me," I commanded, feeling in control now, pushing my mound against his lips. And he did. And the sensation was the sweetest thing. I felt the moistness of his lips and tongue blend with the wetness of my cunt. I felt his tongue work right into me, more nimble still than his fingers, lapping at me, sucking my juices from me. I was in ecstasy, moaning with pleasure and delight, not caring where I was, who might see me, no longer afraid. If this was danger then I wanted it to the max. His hands kneaded both breasts as I grinded away against his tongue. I could feel my release was close now, and I was ready. His tongue could fuck me into oblivion for all I cared, but then, suddenly he stopped.

"No, please, you must finish," I begged.

"What, and let you have all the pleasure. Dream on, woman. I picked you up. I'm giving you the lift. Time for you to return the favour."

I dropped onto his lap, keeping myself aroused by rubbing against the denim of his jeans. Pushing my arse back I leant forwards and opened his belt, pulling it through the belt loops. Then I started on the buttons. His cock was straining for release. He could hardly say there was no pleasure for him in pleasing me. Not if the size of his erection was anything to go by. I opened the buttons slowly, looking up at his face. His eyes were closed, he was biting his lip. He was enjoying this. I put my face down, ready to take his cock into my mouth as soon as it was released from his boxers. First I licked the tip, tasting the tiny droplets of come that rested there, both sweet and salty. He shivered, I assume with pleasure. Then I took the length of him into my mouth. He raised his arse, both to push himself deeper into me, and to pull his jeans and boxers down. Now I could cup his balls as he had my breasts. I felt them tighten in my hand. His orgasm was close too. He groaned. I moved my head back, then down again, increasing my speed, and, judging by the noises he made, his pleasure. Then I felt his hand run along my slit again, his fingers first inside me, then rubbing my clit. I pressed against him and our rhythms soon matched. This was so fucking good. It didn't matter to me where we were, or even who he was. He was giving me so much pleasure I didn't care. Together we pulled away from each other, just in time.

"I'm going to fuck you properly now," he said, pulling a condom over his throbbing cock.

"Good," I replied as I lowered myself onto him slowly, feeling his cock fill me more satisfyingly than his fingers had. Again we moved together, immediately in stride with each other. He held and rocked my hips, my clit rubbed against him. I was going to come now, this time it would be unstoppable. My body began trembling with pleasure. He took my right breast between his teeth, intensifying the moment, that beautiful moment just before the orgasm exploded through me, sending ripples of pleasure first through my cunt, spreading soon throughout my whole body. Just as I felt my release I felt him increase his thrusts. He was close too now, I could tell. I looked down at his face; he was at that moment of surrender. There was no going back for him either. He plunged into me, increasing his rhythm, his cock spurting his seed as his orgasm overwhelmed him. He came to rest on my breasts. I laid my head against his shoulder, as though we were lovers, familiar with each other, not strangers, not even knowing each other's names. My orgasm, though fading now, still pulsed through me, those ebbing shudders extending my pleasure.

"You're good," he said. Then there was silence. We pulled on our discarded clothes as best we could. My jacket just held my top on, and I tugged my skirt over my still throbbing mound, exploring with my fingers that place that had so recently received a good fucking. Taking a sideways glance at him I could see he was doing the same to his cock, obviously reluctant to leave the memory of a good time behind.

We didn't speak on the drive into town. He dropped me by the train station. Just as I was about to get out of the car he pushed his hands between my thighs and thrust one finger deep inside me.

"Still wet, good. Now get out."

I ran my hand over the bulge in his jeans. The bulge that I could see harden and grow.

"Don't worry, I'm going. Thank you for the lift." I slammed the door and he roared away from me.

Five minutes later I opened our front door.

"You're late," accused Jake.

"I know. Sorry."

"Come here. Let me look at you."

I stood in front of him. He was certain to see. Even if my clothes weren't dishevelled and torn he would read the look on my face, spot my bruised, reddened lips. He looked me up and down.

"Was he good?"

I nodded. He pulled me down to straddle his lap.

"Tell me about it, slut, I want every detail," he demanded as he pushed my skirt round my waist, parting my legs further. I tugged at the buttons on his jeans, and dropped my head down. Actions speak louder than words.

Also available from Xcite Books

20 bottom-tingling stories to make your buttocks blush!
Miranda Forbes has chosen only the finest and sauciest tales
in compiling this sumptuous book of naughty treats!
Spanking has never been so popular. Find out why ...

ISBN 9781906125837   price £7.99

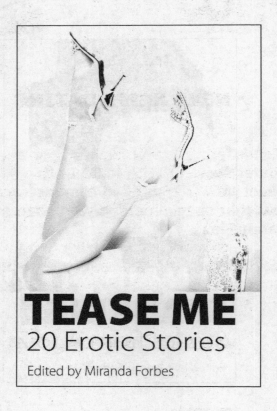

TEASE ME
20 Erotic Stories
Edited by Miranda Forbes

An exciting collection of erotic stories with mixed themes
that are certain to please and tease!

ISBN 9781906125844 price £7.99

NEW! XCITE DATING

Xcite Dating is an online dating and friend-finder service. With Xcite Dating you can meet new friends, find romance and seek out that special person who shares your fantasies.

Xcite dating is a safe and completely anonymous service. Sign-up today – life's too short not to!

www.xcitedating.com

For more information about Xcite Books
please visit

www.xcitebooks.com

Thank you!

Love, Miranda xx